Darwin's Dreams

Also by Sean Hoade

AIN'T THAT AMERICA

Darwin's Dreams

A Novel

Sean Hoade

For Desneé —
Thanks!

CreateSpace • Scotts Valley, CA

Sean Hoade

ISBN 978-1438248073

For Kylara, Ginger, and Alice—
you are my legacy

Are God and Nature then at strife,
    That Nature lends such evil dreams?
    So careful of the type she seems,
So careless of the single life...

— Alfred, Lord Tennyson
In Memoriam, 1850

The *Beagle*, Plymouth, 1831

The problem was Darwin's nose.

Splayed like the blade of a shovel, it was an affront to Captain FitzRoy's phrenological sensibilities. How could he dine with that nose morning, noon, and night? Attend as Darwin tried to wedge it into a snifter of brandy? Watch it roll up and down on the naturalist's face as he chewed, like a Dutch-built tub riding out a hurricane?

This Darwin, who had never sailed farther than a rowboat could take him; this Darwin, who at two and twenty years had only a Bachelor's degree as qualification for the position of naturalist; this Darwin, with his nose as wide and uncultured as those on the cannibals of New South Wales. The principles of physiognomy were as sound as any in science, accepted throughout higher society, and Darwin's nose marked him as a man with whom FitzRoy could not comfortably dine, speak, or socialize.

Did the man suffer from an excess of sensibility and emotion, as his snout indicated? If he was supposed to be so remarkable, why then was his nose not long and slim, as phrenology demanded, as indeed was the captain's own nose? His was a nose utterly suited to its role: to imbue its bearer's countenance with authority and nobility. It was the nose of his ancestors, perhaps becoming even further elongated and slimmer through successive generations of the fine and the worthy.

FitzRoy had looked forward to their first meeting with the greatest anticipation, since this was to be his shipboard friend for an extended expedition. Lord, how he longed for a companion at sea, a worthy companion; but then, with hand extended, that nose had led its owner forward from the shadows, and the captain's face fell like a topsail in a dying breeze.

He had decided right then that he would not allow Darwin to share his cabin; no, he could sling his hammock in the chart room, the one with the mizzenmast rising through its middle. It was expected that they would dine together aboard the *Beagle* the next week, the ship in port as she was being outfitted for her journey, and so the captain formally invited him in front of witnesses. But as he got the words out, he also told Darwin that he would need to bring letters of recommendation attesting to his status as a scientist and as a gentleman if he were to sit at the captain's table. Darwin, to his credit, bowed and assured the captain that he would have them written and sent presently.

A week later, at the writing desk in his cabin, FitzRoy glanced at the letters. To a man, the writers hailed The Nose as a scholar, a fine shooter and collector, and, unmistakably, a gentleman of unimpeachable pedigree.

It was these testimonials that had convinced the captain to accept him at least for one meal, compounded with FitzRoy's need to make haste from England back to Terra del Fuego with the natives he had once so proudly exhibited as new Christians, but who had of late returned to their savage ways, seeking each other out for fornication and perversion. A personal embarrassment, certainly, but potentially more, enough to beach his career on the sharp rocks of public derision. He would need a naturalist to justify the expense of getting the Fuegians out of England, to allow their journey to be deemed a proper scientific and surveying mission.

The unanimity of the letters in support of their man surprised, but somewhat reassured, FitzRoy and so the captain had sent word to Darwin that he would be welcome and expected at six bells in the evening. If the lubber didn't know what that meant, so much the better.

ᎧᎦ   ᎧᎦ   ᎧᎦ

A knock, then silence. On some ships, the steward would simply step into the captain's cabin while knocking, but that level of familiarity had never served on the *Beagle*. FitzRoy waited a few seconds, then called, "Come, Bennett."

"Mister Darwin for dinner, sir." As the steward stepped aside to allow him into the cabin, on deck the watch bell clanged, six times in rapid succession.

FitzRoy stood to greet his guest, suppressing a shudder as the man's face came into full view. Darwin wore a suit with broad lapels, looking fine enough for dinner with the Prince of Wales; FitzRoy appreciated the conscientiousness. They shook hands and dipped their heads in courteous nods. The captain motioned to the table and chairs that Bennett and his mate had already rushed in and set up, amused at Darwin's surprise.

"Won't you take a seat, sir? This should not take long." They sat as Bennett brought glasses and poured from a recent bottle of port. "I understand that you plan to join the clergy. An admirable choice, sir."

Darwin smiled and bowed his head. "And an admirable vessel this is, Captain."

"With her sails off and her masts down, I'm afraid we must make a sorry sight," FitzRoy said, not meaning a word of it.

"Not in the slightest, sir! This noble ship has already sailed the route of my dearest fantasies, and I daresay she looks ready to embark again for even greater glory."

It was flattery, FitzRoy knew it was flattery, but that didn't mean it wasn't true or even that Darwin didn't mean it, and this brought the first smile of the evening to the captain's face. "You are too good."

"And I know of whence I speak," the naturalist said, a finger stabbing the air, "for I have fallen off boats the greater part of my life."

"You say—" FitzRoy started, and his smile vanished. "You sport with me."

"I'm afraid I do not, sir. I am as helpless on the water as a newborn baby." Darwin put his hand to his stomach. "Even the motion of the ship right now makes me a bit uneasy."

"But, sir... the ship is in port—we are lashed to the dock!"

"Yes, I feared that was the case."

FitzRoy sat back in his chair, stunned. The nose told all—before him sat a complete madman "My good man, pray answer me one question: If you are so averse to the water, why then are you in my cabin trying to convince me to take you on a three-year voyage over some of the roughest seas in the world?"

Darwin picked up his aperitif. "Because I will, as you say, enter the clergy upon my final exit from this vessel, whether that is in three years or in three minutes. And I would rather that, when I go to spread the glory of God and His Creation, that I do it having seen as much of it as humanly possible. Sickness may be my constant companion on board, sir, but

Nature shall be my beloved whenever I am off, and your most excellent ship is the conveyance by which I may study her."

Finishing his speech, Darwin lifted the glass to his lips—but FitzRoy put his hand over the rim and called, "Bennett, there! Take this bottle to the gunroom, with my compliments. Then go to my collection and bring up some better port."

"From your *personal* collection, sir?"

"The oldest you can find. Then send a man ashore to get us a fresh chicken, and get Davis working on a pudding."

"What of the salt pork and ship's biscuit then, Captain? You told Cook you wanted that served, sir, to show our guest how——"

"*No*, Bennett, thank you, stay those orders. They were made in jest."

"In jest, sir," Bennett repeated, looking like he had never in life heard anything so utterly lacking in humor.

"That's right. Make this a dinner one can brag about." FitzRoy smiled at his messmate, keeping his gaze away from Darwin's nose. "We have our naturalist."

C3   C3   C3

As they dined, FitzRoy marveled at Darwin. Only four years younger than his own six-and-twenty, he was an entertaining fellow with a full complement of engaging stories, every one of them revealing a man in love with nature, in love with life; a man who would shove a beetle in his mouth if it meant he could grab two more he wanted to collect; a man who kept his intended from becoming upset, when she slipped in mud and stained her dress, by taking a spill himself, even harder, making her laugh instead of cry; a man who would sail around the world for science even though he had become queasy in the jolly-boat bringing him across the placid bay. These anecdotes kept FitzRoy amused all during dinner, but he noticed that although Darwin was often the butt of his own jokes, he never acted the buffoon; all of the comical suffering he encountered was in service of chivalry or wholesome exuberance or intellectual curiosity, always for the greater good. The nose had plainly been broken during one of his well-meaning misadventures, and thus did not signify in terms of physiognomy.

It was an acquired characteristic, not an essential one. He and Darwin could sail together, but more than that, they could be friends.

The pudding finished and their faces red with satiation, FitzRoy waited until Bennett had gone aft, then asked Darwin, "Are you truly that prone to seasickness?"

"I only wish I were exaggerating for humorous effect."

"It is fortunate then that you will be on solid ground more nights than at sea, since you'll be collecting on land while we survey the coast. But I must warn you, my friend: *la mal de mer*, if it is serious enough, will affect your dreams."

A smile attempted to rise, but the gravity of the captain's tone defeated it.

"This is no tale from Coleridge. I know you plan to bring many books aboard—nothing could please me more, I assure you—but whatever you put into your head, the spirals of vertigo will whip into the most vivid images while you sleep.

"I know of a midshipman driven to the edge of sanity by studying spherical trigonometry just before taking to his hammock in a large swell. The resultant seasickness caused him to dream of a world made of nothing but circles, spheres, bubbles of existence."

Darwin nodded earnestly. "Fascinating! I imagine I would dream of disparate worlds and their biologies. Or perhaps philosophies. Aristotle, Leonardo, Lamarck, all have amazing views of natural history—as does the Bible, too, of course."

FitzRoy continued as if the other man had not spoken at all, his eyes fixed on a point somewhere over Darwin's shoulder. "Another vision, one suffered by a junior officer of my acquaintance—before he called upon his own will and dignity not to suffer queasiness, even in the worst typhoon—was that everyone in the world, *everyone*, died a suicide."

The room sagged with silence. Finally Darwin said, "I wonder what the poor boy could have been reading to bring that fantasy about."

"Reading?" FitzRoy seemed to repeat his companion's word from a great distance, finally returning with a shake of his head. "Oh! But I'm afraid I've put a pall over our evening. Please allow me to attend to you on the jolly-boat back, and see if this seasickness is as bad as all that."

Darwin smiled and bowed his head at the kindness. "I have your official invitation to accompany the *Beagle* on her voyage around the world?"

"Certainly, you do."

"Then let us proceed to the boat at your leisure," he said, unable to suppress a tiny chuckle, "and you may see the spectacle for yourself."

ଔ ଔ ଔ

During the two additional weeks it took to outfit the ship and fill her stores for the long voyage, Darwin was thankful the captain allowed him to stay ashore as much as possible; FitzRoy had quickly agreed with Darwin's assessment, saying that never had he seen a man turn so green traveling on a jolly-boat in placid water. This kindness was only one of the reasons Darwin came to see him more as a friend than as an intimidating naval officer, before the *Beagle* even set sail.

But whenever he was on the water, life was a swirling, vertiginous hell.

The brig tacked back and forth off the coast for more than two months, England still in sight as they waited for a favorable wind to begin their journey around the world. Standing to, back and forth, over and over, in nasty seas. Day after day, then week after week, Darwin lay pale and prostrate in his tiny cabin, the immense chart table pinning him into a corner, a drawer removed from the cabinet to make room for his lubber's feet. Standing was an impossibility; all he could do was read and sleep.

And dream.

Aristotle

In this world, Aristotle is right. The characteristics of species are unchanging and essential, their continued existence assured because the universe is moving constantly towards a final purpose that must be fulfilled, its *telos*.

This world is a crowded place, a teeming hell, because as long as a species has a purpose to realize, it cannot go extinct. Giant saurians tromp through the forest, feasting on dodos and sheep, fighting with elephants and mastodons for territory left unoccupied by humans, a small area because human cities include suburbs for *Homo erectus*, ghettos for tool-using *Homo habilus*, sprawling shantytowns from which *Australopithecines* can hunt and gather. Food is scarce, and many individuals of every kind of animal die of starvation—but nothing dies off, not until it has done its duty. Every living thing, from the gnat to the human to the Blue Whale, is eternally hungry.

Religion focuses exclusively on trying to influence the Prime Movers, the forty-seven or fifty-five—their prescribed number differs by sect—intelligent beings behind all change, and the only beings who know for certain the *telos* of every species. People pray to these *primum mobiles*, sacrifice for them, channel their spirits, and prophesize their actions, all to convince these gods to lighten the Earth's load by bringing some classes of creatures to their ends. But the Prime Movers remain unconcerned with, perhaps even unaware of, the existence and lives of humans, let alone hear their prayers. They concern themselves only with moving the multivariate qualities and quantities of the universe in pursuit of its final goal. Their essential nature is to move, not to listen, and it brings religion into conflict with science.

Biology—indeed all science—consists of attempts to discern the *telos* behind each element of the natural world. If a species' purpose can be deduced, then humans desperate for space and food can work to help the creatures fulfill it, and thus hurry them along to extinction, opening more resources for those that remain.

Aristotelian biologists prove that cobras, no matter what else they may happen to do in their lifetimes, whatever else they hunt or kill, in their essence exist only to destroy the mongoose—so hunting the mongoose becomes humanity's job. It takes decades, but when every mongoose has been destroyed, every one, the cobras die off, their *telos* satisfied. A victory for science.

But the world is shaken by news from an expedition to Africa: the discovery of the ratel, which naturalists describe in their journals as an insatiable predator of the cobra. With the cobras gone, how can ratels continue to exist, since what was thought to be the species' essential purpose, the elimination of cobras, has been fulfilled? It is a perplexing anomaly in the biologists' paradigm—until another naturalist expedition returns from Africa with more detailed descriptions of the ratel, journals filled with drawings of the animal hunting certain breeds of rats and particular kinds of birds, even raiding the hives of honeybees, earning them the nickname "honey badger."

Biologists and philosophers wring their hands: Can a species' essence contain multiple purposes? And if only one of those several purposes is fulfilled—in other words, if the cobra has been totally eliminated but the ratel's other essential prey has not—is the species' total *telos* considered unsatisfied?

Postal packets from Africa confirm their worst fears: Baby cobras have been sighted. With their predator still extant, the cobras have come back, because they remain necessary to some part of the badgers' multipartite *telos*.

Biologists and philosophers argue: How many facets might this one species contain? The ratels are voracious carnivores, but which of their killings are fulfillment of their purpose, and which are just historical accidents? Are there such things as historical accidents in a natural world governed by purpose?

Ultimately, it doesn't matter—the Queen funds the Royal Geographic Society to mount a massive hunt of *all* known prey of the honey badger, to scour the Dark Continent and kill every animal it uses for food. Its purpose *must* be destruction of one or more of these species, as the cobra's was to eliminate the mongoose.

The fleet of ships, laden with weapons, traps, and hunters, crawls down the coasts of Europe, then spreads out along Africa, and at Greenwich noon on 23 May, they invade. They torch the jungle, use the newest scientific gadgetry to locate the target animals, then use the latest in weaponry to eliminate them thoroughly.

The hunt spreads into India, the Orient, South America, Australia. No matter what his individual features, every member of mankind comes together to destroy the prey of the ratel, and thus fulfill the species' final purpose and bring it to extinction, clearing up another parcel of the world's booty for Man to enjoy.

Months into the hunt, when regular packets bring news of glorious success after success, the Queen herself attends a lecture on the habitat and characteristics of the soon-to-be-extinct animal, the honey badger, the ratel. Its many species of prey are delineated—the listing of which brings chuckles to the room, since half the named animals have now been confirmed as smoked out and rendered extinct—its sleeping and hunting and mating habits, everything biology has come to understand about how it goes about satisfying its *telos*.

The conclusion of the lecture brings warm applause from all in attendance, but the room falls silent when the Queen, a troubled look on her face, raises a finger and speaks. "My dear Doctor, a question, if you please."

"Of course, Your Highness."

"This animal is a prodigious hunter, but what predators has he?"

The lead naturalist bows his head slightly and says, "The ratel's only natural enemy is Man, Your Highness. They are too tough, too vicious for any other animal to claim them as its prey."

The Queen tucks in her chin and weighs this for a moment. Finally she speaks again. "So no other animal than Man may call it its purpose to hunt and eliminate the ratel?"

"That is correct, Majesty."

"Thus, if the ratel's *telos* is satisfied and it goes extinct, then that purpose of Man's—to eliminate this animal—has been satisfied for him. Yes?"

A paralyzed silence descends. "Again, yes, Majesty."

"And of course, no animal exists that fulfills its purpose by predating on Man," she speaks, her voice tremulating as no one has heard it do before. "How, may I ask, do we know that it is not *Man's telos* to render this animal extinct?"

"Your Majesty, that's..." the naturalist begins, but stops himself short, his face flickering with confusion, then fear. "Man is the highest of the animals... one must assume that he has the highest... at least a higher..."

The Queen shuts her eyes. "May God remember us."

Antemeridian

Their heads bubble with thoughts, as each comes to the surface and changes the shape of its thinker's skull. There is no need for speech; emotions and ideas are reflected physically, and can be read by all.

I wear a soft wool hat pulled down round my ears, so that the phrenologists cannot tell what I am thinking. If I think scientifically, my frontal lobe bulges with causality, and the phrenologists will know I believe nothing of their "science"; if I allow myself to feel my anger towards them, the area just above my ear throbs and pulsates and they will know and can thwart me; if I love or hate or feel the presence of God in His creations, the phrenologists will know.

No one has hair here. If you have nothing to hide, then why are you hiding it?

It is too late—their eagle eyes have espied my secretiveness towards them and their ways. They can see the lump forming on the side of my head, even under the hat, and they are coming for me.

I am caught, and they take me to the guillotine, and cut off my head. Immediately the phrenologist pulls it from the basket, feels all around it for the telltale bumps of thought and personality, and, feeling none, pronounces me dead.

The *Beagle*, at sea, 1832

The captain himself poured Darwin a coffee, the better to warm him up after his dip into the ocean. His hand shook from laughing, and he had to try a few times before he could get the hot liquid into the cup.

"If I had not seen it with my own eyes, I would scarcely have believed it," Darwin said, and had to wait until his own laughter stopped before taking a sip of the coffee and continuing, "Captain FitzRoy, dressed up as the King of the Sea, dunking poor and unsuspecting crew members in paint and pitch, then throwing them overboard!" He had to put his cup down to get through the next fit.

FitzRoy pounded the table in mock gravity and spoke in an unnaturally deep tone: "Neptune spares no man who crosses his Equator. Especially not naturalists too young to shave!"

This sent them into another round of hysterics. "I'm glad you filled a sail with water instead of pouring us into the deep," Darwin said. "I do believe some of your new crew members cannot swim."

"Most of them," FitzRoy said, and tipped a bit more whiskey into their coffees. "I daresay, if a ship's crew *has* to know how to swim, then their captain is a sorry sot indeed." He tapped his cup against Darwin's and they drank, the hysteria leveling out and leaving them with a happy glow.

"They call me 'Hot Coffee,' you know," FitzRoy said after a contented while.

"Who does?" Darwin asked, but only out of courtesy: He had heard it himself several times.

"My crew, my able but very silly crew. 'Hot Coffee,' because I boil over easily. You see?"

"Very clever."

"Yes, yes. I anger very easily, my dear Philosopher, when my station or standing has received an affront. But we are all Christian men, are we not?" He paused for a moment. "Except for the odd Jew or Mohammedan, of course. But we must all live together on this brig, is my point. So sometimes I bring myself down to their level and let them see that I am a man with flaws, just as they are."

"Which is why King Neptune himself ended up soaking wet by the end."

FitzRoy nodded, smiling, and Darwin thought he had never seen anyone so noble. When they had met the year before, the captain seemed to be a man who was born above all others and would remain there for life; but sometimes he let Darwin in to see the man working hard to keep everything together, inside and out, and that made Darwin love him all the more.

"I've been having..." he started, but checked himself from saying the last word, "dreams." FitzRoy allowed him to witness his own humanity, and had warned him himself about how dreams could be brought on by *la mal de mer*, but that didn't mean that the captain wanted to hear Darwin's midnight flights of fancy.

"You've been having...? What, my friend?"

"I've been having…" *Dreams. The oddest dreams.* "… thoughts. About Fanny."

"Ah, your darling Fanny. Not the most patient of young ladies."

Darwin hadn't meant to say her name again—hadn't meant *ever* to say it again—but it was all he could think of, and now he saw that this was because it was in fact all he could think of, Fanny married to that doltish politico. "She promised she would wait."

"Ah, stiff upper lip, Darwin." FitzRoy leaned in closely. "May I be candid?"

"Of course."

"The seafaring life is not one for the married. There are too many temptations to break the sacred vow when we're in port. It's really much better being a bachelor. Not being married, you can do what a man must, and be none the worse off for it, morally."

"Do you mean… visiting women? Who receive money?" Darwin could feel his cheeks flushing as he said this, and felt like a ninny and a prude.

"I'm afraid so," FitzRoy said seriously. "You're not a clergyman yet, are you? How ever will you instruct your congregation in how to wash away their sins when you haven't gotten yourself soiled enough yourself to know?"

Darwin stared at the captain, dumbfounded, his eyes unblinking as he searched for something, anything, to say in reply.

Before he could, however, FitzRoy's face broke into a huge grin, unable to contain his joke any longer. "I am sorry, Darwin—oh, ha, ha—but I couldn't resist seeing your face—*ha! ha! ha! ha!*—when… when…" But it was hopeless; FitzRoy collapsed into a fit of delighted cackles and could speak no more.

Darwin sat up straighter in his seat, projecting a hurt dignity—but with a belying half-smile that only made FitzRoy laugh harder. "I believe that I am in the company of an expert in the area of pranks and follies," he said, joining the captain in chuckling now. "So this is my return for confessing my deep romantic wounds."

"Oh, my dear Darwin, it did take your mind away from treacherous Fanny for a few moments, did it not?"

In amazement, Darwin realized that the joke had done just that, and tipped his cup in admiration. FitzRoy wasn't just a friend; he was a marvel.

Still, as he drank and looked with appreciation at his captain, he was glad he had not said anything about the nature of his nighttime visions. For the dreams were strange, but they were wonderful, and he would not have been able to share a derisive chuckle over them, no matter how ridiculous they may have seemed.

The Ark

The mastodon's cry is like a blast from a rusty trumpet, sharp but ragged.

The frightened glyptodont snuffles around in the middle of its shrinking island, fear bunching its plates of armor as high as a man's head.

The giant deer twitches slightly in its otherwise frozen stance, trapped by the rushing water as it watches animal after smaller animal climb up the planks and through the door of the Ark.

It is the Flood of forty days and forty nights, and Noah brings aboard seven pairs of every clean species, two of every unclean, from the lowliest insect to the most magnificent lion. But even he, as he shepherds the saved aboard, looks out with sadness upon the two kinds of animals he cannot save: those too skittish to board the Ark, and those too large to fit through its door. The other humans, too frightened of the huge animals to challenge them for their land, have already drowned.

"Noah," his wife, Na'amah, speaks softly to him, "the Lord must know that He has forsaken these beasts. It is not your doing."

Noah puts a hand on his wife's. "Men will wonder what became of these creatures. Why they, among all the creatures, were not given refuge aboard this vessel."

The saber-toothed tiger curls into its sleeping position, ignoring the unicorn a few feet away that scrapes in despair at the wet earth. Even the tiger sees there is no point in eating when death is moments away.

The gryphon and the chimæra climb to the highest point in the tallest trees and watch with their golden eyes as the water swirls around the trunks below.

"The beautiful, the hideous, they are doomed as one," Noah says with a sigh as he draws up the planks and closes the door, the hopelessly small door. "God must have a reason. He must."

Na'amah takes his shoulders and leads him away from the door. The Ark is floating now, moving away from what little land is left, teeming with all the life it can hold. One more creature could not fit, let alone two of a kind. Na'amah shows this to her husband, then lets him weep at her breast. "God is good," she says.

The ship creaks as it rides the waves, which pass and inundate the shore. An anguished roar from land pierces the sound of water and wood. Noah knows what the sound is, and it makes him weep anew.

It is Megalosaurus, water lapping at her feet, the saurian mother screeching for her eggs as they are seized and swallowed by the merciless sea.

Antemeridian

Why is the chamber pot in my cabin once again? I wonder, and rise from my hammock to move it. But there squats the Captain, grunting. He fixes me with eyes narrowed against the effort. "Darwin, you fugger, what have you done to me?"

I don't say anything, instead just slowly approach the Captain and reach out for the brass pot, although he still wrenches his stomach in the throes of some ungodly cramp. Quick like a cat, I snatch the pot and look into it.

It is half-filled with huge gold coins. For some reason, this is what I expected.

"Look what you have done to me!" the Captain cries, and I see him rush out of the cabin and hear him clamber up the steps to his quarters. "Bloody seasick *fugger!*"

The chamber pot grows heavy in my hands, and when I look down at it again, it is about to overflow with the doubloons, the shiny metal clinking as it multiplies.

I drop the pot, and it breaks right through the planks of the deck, shattering the wood of each level, creating a cloud of splinters in the deck below, and below, and below, until—

An aortic fountain of sea water bursts up through the holes until it rushes into my cabin and breaks through the top bulkhead. Shouts and screams for Chips, the carpenter, but already I can feel the ship creaking and starting to go under—the waterline outside has risen almost level with my porthole.

The Captain, shoving panicked sailors out of the way, rushes back down the steps and again into my cabin, his brass-bound breeches pooled around his ankles. "Stand back—for the good of Christ, stand back!" he bellows, and leans his bottom over the gusher. He strains, and a flood of heavy gold coins rains from his arse. They are massive, bigger than any South American shield of the sun, and fill the ballast compartment, blocking the water. Then the lowest levels of the ship are filled completely with the golden mass, and the water is forced out. The ship rises in the sea.

Screaming "Look what you've done, fugger!" again and again the Captain shits and shits his mountain of gold, until the ship is overflowing with money, buoyant, and lifts out of the water completely, rising into the sky, up and up and finally gone.

The *Beagle*, Salvador, Brazil, 1832

As Darwin was handed up the side of the ship from the jolly-boat, Captain FitzRoy took his hand himself and pulled him aboard. "My God, man, what's happened to you? You're white as new muslin. Did you not find the specimens you had wished for?"

"Indeed I did, Captain; they are in the boat below."

"Then what—" But he stopped himself. His first job was to comfort his friend, not to satisfy his own prurient curiosity. "Come to my cabin and let us have a dram—Bennett, there! Bring our Philos to my quarters and set him up, will you? I shall be along presently."

When his coxswain had led Darwin away, FitzRoy leaned over the side and called down to the men in the jolly-boat as discreetly as possible, "Mister Covington, report there! What has become of Mister Darwin?"

Covington stood from the crate of specimens, which looked to FitzRoy to be all manner of rocks and stones, something he could not see the need for on his ship. Still—another time for that, he reminded himself. "After naturalizing in the forest, sir," Covington said, hesitating slightly, "he saw something upon coming onto the beach."

"That is to be expected if his eyes were open, Mister Covington. What sight was it that has disconcerted him so?"

The young man paused before muttering, "He's a Whig, you know, sir."

"And I a Tory. Now, is this a report or is it a conversation? Get on with it before I have the cat brought out."

Covington nodded, steeling himself. "Mister Darwin witnessed a Black being... corrected, sir. Speaking of the cat."

FitzRoy shut his eyes. A Liberal who had never been out of Britain, seeing for the first time the flogging of a slave... he doubted very much that Darwin would understand the need for such unflinching discipline, even in an unruly place such as South America. "Very good, Mister Covington. Mind your mates take care with his important—*things*."

The captain straightened his hat, tugged his coat a bit more snug around his shoulders, and proceeded to the aid of his friend, the person to whom he had grown most close on the months of their voyage thus far. This was his compatriot; he would give him his full sympathy and understanding.

ભ   ભ   ભ

The half-hour bell had not yet rung again when the entire ship shook.

"*Do not presume to quote Scripture at me!*" Fitzroy shouted with a voice usually reserved for being heard over full-tilt fusillades. "It does not matter if you are to enter the clergy upon your return—a man of *your* station will *not* speak condescendingly to a captain of the Royal Navy!"

"Robert, I—"

"You will address me as *Captain FitzRoy* or you will not address me at all! You have become all too familiar in your dealings with me."

Darwin recalled the captain's insistence that he be called "friend" or "Robert" when they were in the privacy of his cabin, but said nothing except, "Captain FitzRoy, sir, I meant only to point out that while the Bible does casually mention slavery, even to the point of seeming to endorse it, nowhere does it call for men's torture and humiliation at the hands of brutes and killers."

"*Casually* mention it? St. Paul himself turned an escaped slave away and sent him back to his rightful master. That is as good as blessing it."

"But Paul also told the master that he must keep his responsibilities."

"Of course! Men are always to take care of their property."

"Property! My dear Captain, could our loving God truly mean for some men to be *owned* by others? Even if this evil arrangement is, as you say, acceptable under the laws of men, I cannot believe it is so under the laws of God."

Coldly, FitzRoy said, "The trade, if it is evil, is a necessary one for the glory of our Empire, and also it brings Salvation to these poor souls, something which they had no chance of finding as savages wandering naked in Africa." His delicate features were now aswirl with red, which made his newly becalmed tone seem all the more chilling. "You will not lecture me, Mister Darwin. I know my Bible."

"But you are satisfied to follow only the parts that suit you," Darwin said—and regretted it immediately, even before FitzRoy had leapt to his feet with new rage.

"*And you, sir, are never to sit at my table again!* Now kindly comport yourself to your own quarters before I have the Marines escort you to shore and *leave you there with your bugs and your carcasses!*"

A retort danced at the very edge of Darwin's tongue, but he swallowed it. Instead, he bowed curtly and exited the room.

The captain was a good and moral man; he just didn't know the Book the way Darwin did, and it showed in the aristocratic way he defended the interests of Man over those of Nature and God. Besides, the man had a right to his own opinion, especially on his own ship—

Brig, he reminded himself as he trundled up the ladder to the poop, trying daily to become more nautical. *The* Beagle *is a double-masted* brig. It *was* a ship, of course; but he had been told by more than one crewman that it was more accurate and seamanlike to refer to it as a "brig." Not that it mattered anymore; obviously he would be getting off when they put in once again, and finding his own way back to England.

And his imminent exile notwithstanding, he still argued the point in his mind—for who had ever said that a man had the right to his own opinion about moral matters, matters of God's justice, just because he knew how to hoist a sail? *Don't quote Scripture at me*, indeed. The man was a god upon the water and a devil everywhere else.

Darwin did comport himself back to the chart room, which had never seemed so small, and bent double against the nausea caused by the movement of the boat—the ship—the *brig*. The movement of the brig.

He muttered an oath, and moved to the hammock. Through trial and error, mostly the latter, he had finally realized that one could not enter a hammock with his feet placed first. That would end with a naturalist upon the floor—*deck*— and a curious captain in the cabin just below. No, now he placed his fundament into the belly of the beast, as it were, and allowed himself to be cradled, turning to the correct alignment within the hammock as he did so.

There. Just in time to be cast ashore, he was becoming a thorough seaman.

Now that he was in place, however, he found that the book he had been reading—Paley's *Natural Theology*—was still on the edge of the chart table, just beyond his fingertips. He stretched to reach it, and with the help of the ship's rocking was able to brush the spine.

He added a bit of his own weight to the slight swing of the hammock, and allowed the ship's movement to bring him back. Again he reached, and this time just nudged the book, his fingers not quite in place to grasp it. The next pass would do it.

More weight, more momentum added to the pendulum, and this time he clutched the book by stretching his body as far to the edge as it would go and clamping his thumb and forefinger like a vise around the binding. *Success!*

But he had overreached, and the hammock turned and bulged convex and spat him and his book onto the deck, leaving him crumpled in a painful, nauseated heap. In this position, with his journey truncated, his vision of a kind Empire in tatters, his shoulder aching from the tumble, Darwin wept. For the Salvation of his friend, for his own foolish pride, for the long trip back home with nothing but empty hands.

He wiped his eyes, then leaned on the chart table to bring himself back to his feet, brushing off his coat and trousers with his palms. Then he picked up the Paley and placed himself back into the hammock, adjusting perfectly to keep it level and accommodating.

He had barely cracked the book when there came three sharp knocks on the door. "If that is one of the Marines, please note that I am unarmed."

The door swung open and Robert FitzRoy stepped in, his hat in his hands.

"Captain!" Darwin started, almost capsizing once again.

"Mister Darwin—no, please, no need to rise—I need only to ask you…" FitzRoy paused, then straightened his back and stiffened his lip. "May I ask of you a favor?"

Darwin settled back. "I am yours, sir."

"I ask only that you accept my apology. It is offered sincerely."

"Nothing would make me happier—as long as you will accept mine as well."

A smile broke out under the captain's wispy moustache. "I agree to your terms."

"A most gentlemanly surrender."

"Indeed." FitzRoy placed his hat back upon his head and bowed. "After your rest, you will be most welcome at dinner. And Darwin—Charles—you will address me as *Robert*, or you will not address me at all."

With a smile, Darwin nodded, and the captain took his leave, leaving his naturalist to marvel at the ebb and flow of his friend's emotions. As hot as coffee, it was true, and just as bracing. After a few minutes of staring at the closed door, he once again opened his book but, exhausted inside and out, drifted into sleep after running his eyes over just a couple of lines.

Paley

In this world, any level of complexity is due to conscious, intelligent design.

The port hugs the shoreline of the bay, docked ships being loaded with bags of grain carried by Negroes on the tops of their heads. Nearby, the naturalist walks with bare feet, enjoying the cool foam racing across his toes as the surf breaks on the beach. Tiny stones, churned up from the floor of the bay, are spread before him by the waves, and as they retreat it is only with care that he avoids treading on them.

The stones are smooth, polished by many centuries of contact with the water. The naturalist pauses and bends to select one especially shiny specimen. How very much it looks like a bauble buffed by a gem-smith to its finest luster, all the better to catch the eye of a lady walking by his shop window. Its design is simple, but reveals its divine origins by its beauty. Amused, he tosses the stone back into the bay.

A new sheet of tide rushes over his feet, and when it recedes, another tiny stone has been deposited before him. But no—it isn't a stone at all, but a shell! Delighted, the naturalist crouches and picks it up carefully. It has no occupant; it is as a fossil on a mountain, lifeless, although it has remained until now under the sea, where its creature had once lived. It was a home to that animal, but was also formed by the animal itself. A brilliant idea, only one of God's infinite series. He stands and tosses the shell into the water, hearing as he does so the cry of one of the slaves loading the ships.

He fixes his sharp gaze the few hundred yards away to the dock and sees a whip come down across the back of a Negro held fast against a railing by chains. The white man with the whip lashes the slave a dozen times, while all on the dock and the ship go about their business. There are no women at the port at this time, no squeamish midshipmen, and no one but the naturalist seems alarmed at the display.

The man with the whip motions to two of the other Negroes to release the whipped man, who collapses onto his knees, untended even by his fellow slaves, who fear the whip themselves. In half an hour, before the naturalist has wound his way to the port, the man is back at work, toiling under his load, his back still wet with blood.

The work continues, the waves still crash, and the tide yet dredges from the bay.

Carried by the rushing water, a lock of seaweed curls around the naturalist's ankle. Dark and briny, the broken piece of plant is the perfect food for hundreds, perhaps thousands, of diverse species. The naturalist smiles as he unbends it from his leg and examines its cellulose structure. The cellulose itself is innutritious, indigestible to any animal, but absolutely necessary as a framework for the edible components to be made available to the creatures that ingest it. The naturalist sniffs the plant and with a smile shakes his head; he doubts he could ever find such a thing palatable at all, let alone the basis of his diet. Amazing that its connoisseurs are lucky enough to live under the sea, he thinks, or would be amazing, if God had not designed it exactly that way.

Another wave, another discovery, this time a small fish deposited at the naturalist's feet, heaving and twitching for air. Instantly he scoops it up—taking time for the tiniest of examinations to see that it is a common carp, nothing he need make a note of or bring back to the ship—and delivers him back into the water. He smiles at his own compassion, but also at the fact that there is nothing but air in the atmosphere above the ocean, but this air is useless to the carp, since the fish must strip it from the water through its gills. That is how it was made, another miracle. Things so designed are a source of happiness to the naturalist, filling his breast with faith and confidence. For a system to work, the Lord must put it into His plan; nothing complex can be, unless He blesses its workings with His design.

Lost in his musings, the naturalist is startled when the crack of rifle-shot rends the air. He jumps at the sound, only to see the beaten slave running up the beach towards him; his master leans over the railing and squeezes off another volley, but the Negro has outrun the shooter's range.

The naturalist steps out of the escapee's path; he would be unable to stop the much larger man even if he were disposed to aid an inhuman slaver. But breaking forth from the dock come three huge Negroes, sending up arcs of sand as they race after their compatriot, past the onlooker, and in what seems like seconds they have caught him and forced his face into the wet. They stand him up and lead him back towards the dock, his head hanging in defeat.

The waves rush over the naturalist's feet once again, and he looks down as he feels something hard tap against the metatarsal of the rightmost toe of his right foot. The waves have deposited a gleaming gold pocket-watch, ticking as if it were just put together by its maker. An even more complex design than shells and fishes, to be sure! But, still astounded by the complicity of the slaves in returning the runaway to his angry master, the naturalist takes no interest in the intricate gears and springs of the machine. It cannot reproduce; it has no natural habitat; its intricacy holds no mystery. God would not waste His time on such things, would not design such works. The systems and devices of Man must be anathema to Him, or at the very least beneath His notice. And if that were not true, then the naturalist would rather believe there is no God at all than believe in One who is in equal part trivial and cruel.

Antemeridian

I sit in an oak tree, a hundred feet from the ground, the branches swaying in the breeze. My father is with me; he is an eagle perched a few yards away, so he can keep an eye on both myself and its huge, scraggly nest.

"You hold on to those twigs for dear life," the eagle says with disdain. "Do you think no one can see you? For Jesus' sake, boy, let them go."

"I'll fall."

"If you fall, stretch your wings and catch a draft back up." The eagle leans forward and lets itself fall, dropping twenty feet before reaching out and riding the wind to place him in exactly the spot he left. "You see? It's what eagles do."

But I only look at my hands, which are hands, not talons; and my body, which is wrapped in a waistcoat and breeches, not adorned with feathers. I mutter weakly, "I am not an eagle, Father."

"I can see that for myself! Now fall, or I'll push you off."

Heads peek out from the nest now. His brother Erasmus, his sister Caroline, their mother, the neighbors, Josiah Wedgwood and his daughters, FitzRoy, a Dragoon soldier, a stuffed dragon, the Mayor of Shrewsbury, all of them staring at me, unblinking, with their black bird eyes.

"Fall, Bobby. I'm a physician, remember."

"You're an eagle."

At that, the eagle makes good on his threat, hopping over to me and pecking out a chunk of flesh from my back, ripping a hole through my coat. I cry out and let go of the branch, dropping immediately out of sight of the burning eyes and hitting limb after limb of the tree on my way to the ground. The branches snap, my bones snap, and when I reach the ground, the final branch whirls me around before setting me gently on my feet.

"Stellar!" my father calls from the treetop. "Now fly back up!"

"I—I can't! My arms are broken!"

A grunt of frustration from above, and then the eagle flies out and carves an arc through the air, coming to a halt at the ground in front of me. "What do you want from me, then?"

"Fix my arms? You are a physician."

"I am an eagle." It preens for a moment, ruffling its neck feathers, then regards me again, coolly. "But let me see what can be done."

I lie on the grass and watch the hundreds of birds hop down, from branch to branch, the tree groaning under the shifting weight. My father pecks out a piece of flesh from my arm, then another, then another, everyone watching as I writhe and scream under his care.

Bahia Blanca, Argentina, 1833

"I don't believe I have spent a full week out of sight of the sea since I was twelve years old," FitzRoy said with a rueful smile, taking a rest from the hike to look out over the valley. "For once I am thankful that ships are made of wood that rots and must be replaced."

Darwin chuckled and translated the captain's words to the curious *gauchos* who led them on the trail. They guffawed in appreciation, although they would have had no idea why a sea captain should be happy about such a thing, the mountains being as monotonous to them as the airless doldrums were to sailors. Darwin was glad simply to be off the rocking ship, which caused him dreams far stranger than anything he would have expected from simple seasickness. On land, at least, his sleep had remained blissfully blank.

"Your bags of rocks and bones are severely testing our poor *burro*," FitzRoy said lightly. "Could we perhaps *draw* a few of them instead of dragging them about with us?"

"I'm afraid I am not much of an artist. I wish Mister Martens had come."

"With revolution in the air—what do they call it? *Revuelta?*"—the *gauchos* both looked back at them at the sound of the words—"I thought it would be safer to keep our party to a minimum." Darwin nodded, glancing with regret at the struggling *burro*, and FitzRoy startled him by shouting, "But blast Martens! You have in your company one of the finest naturalist artists in the Navy!"

Darwin laughed with pleasure. "Of course! I must admit that I had forgotten entirely your charcoals of the Fuegians in their natural habitat. I would be most happy to lighten this poor animal's load."

Delighted, FitzRoy had Darwin call for the *gauchos* to stop and rest while he pulled his sketchbook and pencils from the pack, tools he had brought in the hope that he could assist Darwin—who, for all his brilliance with rocks, was indeed a hopeless artist.

"Pick your pleasure, whatever you might like to leave behind," FitzRoy said, settling himself against a boulder near the trail. "I am entirely yours."

But Darwin surprised the captain by pulling out and unwrapping a large, striated stone and saying, "This one, I think."

"Do you not want to save the rocks and leave the skeletons? I thought you were interested primarily in the geology here."

"The geology is fascinating, but over the course of the past few days I have found fossils of animals I cannot identify. I thought I should bring them back and—"

FitzRoy stood and marched to the *burro*'s pack, an expectant smile lifting one side of his mouth. "Show me, if you please. I believe I can be of service here as well."

Darwin kept his eyes on the captain for a few seconds, then let out a breath and pulled one of the large, carefully wrapped fossils from the pack, handing it gingerly to FitzRoy, who carefully laid it upon the ground and unwrapped it.

"Ah, I see… you have a member of *rodentia* here. Note the dentition, and the well-developed pterygoid region. Yes, it is a rodent, although I admit of unusual size."

"Unusual size? The skull is as big as a dog's!" Darwin said with a laugh. "But more important than that, even if it is an entirely new species, is *where* it was found."

"*Where*? You and Covington were digging not twenty paces from our tent."

"Yes, but this skull—this whole fossil of a large land mammal, obviously of great antiquity—was to be found only under a layer of fossilized seashells."

FitzRoy marveled at this. "Is it some sort of… mammalian amphibium?"

"The rest of the skeleton does not seem to indicate that, no."

"Then how could its fossils be under those of sea creatures? The Flood, perhaps?"

"That is the usual explanation for shells on top of mountains, of course, but if there is to be a scientific explanation made…" He watched for the captain's nod, then continued, "I'm afraid a sketch wouldn't do this kind of anomaly justice. Besides, I have the rest of it wrapped in the pack and ready to be analyzed." Darwin patted the heavy bag, which was enough to make their animal shift his feet.

"No wonder our *burro* is thinking of joining the *resistencia*." The idea of a rebel *burro* stretched a smile across FitzRoy's face—until he saw that one of the *gauchos* had stood and was now stalking towards them, his machete pulled out of its sling.

"*¿Hay un problema?*" Darwin asked as he rapidly rewrapped the skull and jammed it back into the pack. "There's no problem here. *No hay problema aqui.*"

The *gaucho* narrowed his eyes and said something in Spanish so rapidly that FitzRoy wondered how even another Argentinean could understand it. The man's stare was murderous, and his hand gripped the machete more tightly. Darwin's rifle was on the *burro*, but FitzRoy saw that the *gaucho* could shoot him down before he even got the first buckle undone. If this revolutionary and his friend, who had to be personally persuaded by *el general* to escort FitzRoy, Darwin, and their jobs man Covington across the rebellious territory, decided to kill them, there wasn't a thing they could do to save themselves. The *gaucho* leaned in closer to Darwin and let loose with another cannonade of angry gibberish.

But Darwin... laughed. The madman *laughed*, and after a few seconds—here FitzRoy literally blinked and rubbed his eyes—the *gaucho*'s angry gaze broke, first just in amazement, and then into a disbelieving grin, and then with unmistakable laughter as the huge man was reduced to tears.

"My God, Darwin, what did you do?" FitzRoy almost yelled as the second *gaucho* came over and heard the naturalist, at the first man's request, repeat his statement. After a another moment, he too doubled over, shaking with mirth.

"They heard you saying *la revuelta* and *la resistencia* when I had told them you knew no Spanish. They thought I was a liar—that we were spies!"

"But... what did you say to render them so hysterical?"

"Waste not another thought about it, my dear. It has disarmed the situation."

"What did you say, man? Tell me!"

Darwin hesitated before finally saying, "I told them that you didn't know any better... the only Portuguese you knew was what you picked up from *as putas*."

"From *what?*" FitzRoy asked, but he knew. He had been a sailor all his life.

"From prostitutes," Darwin said, confirming FitzRoy's surmise. "I had hoped it would strike their funny-bone. It seems my aim was true."

For a moment, FitzRoy was perfectly balanced between horror at being called a whoremonger—even in jest—and relief that the larger of the *gauchos* was sliding his machete back into its sling even as he wiped the tears from his eyes.

"I do apologize, Robert. It certainly wasn't in reference—" Darwin said, but here he had to stop, lest their accompanying crewman believe his captain was partial to joking about prostitutes with clergymen-to-be. "Covington once told me that the Brazilians find the thought of pink-bodied Englishmen *in flagrante delicto* uproariously funny."

"It's true, sir," Covington said, his eyes angled towards the ground.

FitzRoy swallowed. "It—it was good thinking. Saved our skins, so it did."

Darwin nodded, but a silence remained, so he took the massive rodent skull from the pack once again and added brightly, "I rather think I agree with you about the skeleton. Perhaps you could sketch it and—"

"I think not, my friend. I seem to have lost the taste for drawing at the moment. Excuse me," FitzRoy said, and walked up the trail, ahead of the *gauchos*, who were still trying to control their laughter, and over the ridge, out of sight.

Darwin watched him go, but was distracted by the smaller *gaucho* approaching him as if he were an explosive device. "*¡Señor!*" he whispered as loudly as he dared. "*¡No se mueva, señor!*"

Don't move? Darwin translated to himself, and thought: *Why ever not?*

The *gaucho* inched closer, his hand extending to where Darwin's sleeve had been rolled up to his elbow. On his bare forearm, he could see, sat a massive black-and-white-striped insect with a tawny midsection, its shock of bristles extended in a way that suggested great agitation, offense, even anger—

"Robert, I am sorry," Darwin said. The *gaucho* lunged, and the insect—a member of *Heteroptera*, predators all—bit him, stung him, whatever *Heteroptera* did—it was undecided, more research needed to be done—and sent him into a convulsion of pain that knocked him to the rocky ground, straight into unconsciousness.

When he came to, his entire arm throbbing through the crude poultice that had been applied, the sun had gone down and the others had set up camp near where he had fallen.

"My dear Philos," FitzRoy said as soon as his eyes were open, "you have received a most dreadful bite."

"It could be a sting," Darwin slurred. "Need more research."

"You have a high fever. We dared not move you," FitzRoy said, and leaned in close enough to whisper. "The *gauchos*... they keep pointing at where you received your bite—or sting—and then at the insect, repeating, *Malos sueños, malos sueños por sempre*. Do we need to take you back to the ship? To the apothecary's? What do these words mean?"

Darwin searched his mind for the words, and when they finally came to him, he almost wept: *Bad dreams. Bad dreams forever.*

Before he could speak these words to FitzRoy, he slipped away again, and slept.

Leonardo

In this world, Leonardo is right: The human body and the corpus of the Earth are microcosm and macrocosm. Scientists can learn about the history and workings of the planet by studying the physiology of the body, and vice versa, since they are more than analogous—they are a unity. They work the same way, through the interaction of the four elements, earth for heaviness and stability, water for cohesion and circulation, air for movement, and fire for heat.

The fecund Earth is a mother, birthing season after season, eon after eon. She brings forth the animals and plants that clamp to her and suckle from her, growing and thriving in her presence and her care. A mother is a lush Earth, blossoming with spring as her breasts fill, her cheeks redden, and her belly becomes round like the sun appearing over the horizon, giving birth to a new day.

The marine fossils found in the mountains are there because water, the circulatory fluid of the Earth, pushes the remains of sea creatures up and out from the ocean floor as the planet's blood moves into greater altitudes. Silt and dirt are dragged back into the ocean as the blood, having delivered its nutrients, is drawn back down towards the heart of the Earth, its lungs, the ocean.

The lungs breathe, rising and falling every six hours, filling the veins with water as salty as human blood is salty. The humors of the human body are stirred through the breathing of the lungs and the beating of the heart, although each will settle into its natural place at death; so too are the planet's elements circulated, but at its last breath will settle into its natural configuration of heavy earth at the center, the less heavy water above it, then lighter air, then fire, the lightest element, which at death may escape entirely.

The harmony between man's corpus and that of the Earth is repeated as that between the Earth and the body of the Universe. The sun, the heart of the Universe, pulses with vitality and energy that are pushed outward, through the veins of the æther, to nourish the planets and the stars, cycling back in that same invisible substrate. Its elements are the same: earth, in the solidity of planets; water, in the cohesion of gravity; air, in the æther; and fire, in the burning of the stars. It is not an analogy. It is again a unity, a literal reflection from the smaller mirror to the larger.

If these are true, say the clerics, then the corporeal Universe must be a microcosm for the only greater body, the infinite body of God, and this too must be a unity, a concord with the lesser, not some kind of game-player's analogy. But what are His elements? Where is His heart? Can something be said truly to *circulate* if it must travel an infinite distance before returning? These questions are raised in medical school lecture halls, in scientific debates about the nature of fossils, any arena in which the body—be it of Man, Earth, the Universe, or God—is dissected and analyzed.

The most popular conjecture is that God's body is made up of omniscience (earth), omnipotence (fire), infinite love that connects (water), and infinite love that liberates (air). Others say that God is Heaven (air), Earth (earth), and Hell (fire), with the water element binding the realms together. And still others maintain that God must be comprised of time (water), space (air), matter (earth), and consciousness (fire). The idea that God has no body, that Jesus was the body of God and so was made of the same elements working the same as in any other man, is rejected because God can never be microcosm, only macrocosm.

Whatever its proposed makeup, all agree that the body of God must be a unity with its microcosms, its water element flowing as blood flows through a human, as water flows through the Earth, as gravity flows through celestial bodies. This is little more than piffling, savoring that the Godhead operates exactly as does the Universe, the Earth, the body—since it cannot be subject to experimentation or even observation—but it is a way of worshiping all of those at once, especially among scientific gentlemen.

It is in this atmosphere of enjoyable speculation that someone kills God.

A bill nailed one morning to the door of the Royal Society reads:

"If the body of God is a unity with these other bodies—not in the way of some specious analogy, but a true unity—then we have made God mortal, for the body of man must die, and so its unity the Earth must one day die, and *their* unity the Universe must die. Their pulses must come to rest; their elements will separate and settle; and they will live no more. This is also the ultimate fate of the Lord our God. We have put our faith in a small deity, a God who will die. We have wasted our prayers, sent to a mortal being."

No one knows who posted this thesis, or why. But that hardly matters—the idea is loose, and it shakes every field from geology to astronomy to medicine to theology. It is quickly proposed at Westminster Abbey and at the Royal Society that this "mortal" God revealed by the bill could be but a lesser deity than the one true God, who cannot die. This attempt at correction of the anomaly is undermined, however, by arguments that if there is another God above this mortal one, then He too must be mortal, if He is of a unity with the other parts of His Creation, if Man were truly created in His image.

There is fear in the streets, losses on the stock exchange. The Queen, temporal guardian of His Church, hides in shame for having hired herself out to One so common.

The Church, desperate to save itself, calls on the leading scientific minds of the day to show that the relationship between Man and Earth, between Earth and Universe, is *not* a unity; only in this way, they reason, can they restore God's immortality.

The scientists, funded by the Church, engage in a storm of research and discovery. After a year, they announce that fossils appear on mountaintops because the Earth is of incredible longevity, thousands of millions of years, and what are now mountains were once the bed of an ancient sea. There is no circulatory fluid to the Earth; although there is a "vapor cycle" by which water evaporates from the ocean and is returned to the land in the form of rain. Man's blood does not evaporate and rain down on his head—there is no unity between the two.

And through their researches, astronomers and physicists find that there is no substance called the "æther"—instead, they announce, they have reason to suspect a substanceless void filled only with chunks of matter and electro-magnetic energy. This means that there is no circulation to the Universe; there is no unity with the Earth.

The faithful rejoice, for the research of the Church and science has protected the dignity and sanctity of their immortal God.

But on their knees at night, or sitting in church, many despair, wondering what their Creator must look like, if not like His creations. He is not of a unity with them. To keep God's throne unsullied, His children have been turned into orphans.

Antemeridian

In the mouth of the fœtus of the universe are the buds of first teeth, undetectable as yet but poised to strike out and become stars, spin into galaxies, burst into gases and flame. Here is the prehensile tail, grasping the planets and flinging them on their curled trajectories; here are the gills, breathing the fluid of the æther; here are the webs between fingers and toes, allowing it to swim through the Milky Way.

What is this egg become embryo? What will the universe bear? Rippling through space and time are the kicks of this fœtus, sending waves of Creation to form all the specters of the night sky, a million million million suns.

The monster is ready to break the water of its cosmic mother, to shriek out its existence. It bloodies the walls of the womb as it fights to escape, it pierces—it burns—

It illuminates, this Idea.

Valparaiso, Chile, 1834

"I understand you knew our Darwin at Shrewsbury," Fitz-Roy said over tea in Richard Corfield's sitting room.

"Quite so," said Corfield, a congenial twenty-five-year-old who looked much like Darwin, except his nose was unblemished by misfortune and remained as straight and narrow as a Fuegian's canoe, and he chuckled. "He wasn't then the responsible and learned man you have aboard your ship these days. He liked his shooting and riding even then, but was not much of a reader, I must tell you. His tales of his prodigious reading on the *Beagle* astound me more than does even his amazing long beard."

"While we're at sea, I'm afraid there isn't much for him to do, being as sea-sick as he is on any water. But he is a most estimable reader now, and he applies that knowledge at every opportunity, even to the most ungentlemanly point of winning arguments against his captain."

They shared a laugh, but soon enough the mood turned somber once again. FitzRoy said quietly, "He hasn't stirred today since I've been here."

Corfield instinctively glanced in the direction of the sick-room. "No. The longer he has been here—what is it, several weeks now at the least—the more time he spends in sleep, falling into it from a most unpleasant state of fever and discomfort."

"The physician? What does he say?"

"He is truly perplexed," Corfield said with a shake of his head. "He has theories, but none of his treatments have made a whit of difference to our poor Charles."

FitzRoy barely checked himself from saying *It was that damned bug*, not only because it would have been impolite but also because the only evidence he had was that Darwin had become progressively sicker, on and off, since he had received the nasty bite the year before. Now he had fallen into a swoon and had scarcely come out long enough to talk to his old school mate, let alone return to the ship. "Has Darwin—Charles—said anything himself?"

"He is in the world of dreams and nightmares, I think. I tried to comfort him by relaying how much the learned world is abuzz over the fossils and specimens he has sent to Reverend Henslow—but he cried, 'Fame! I am renowned in time to die.' I allow that this frightened me, to hear a man as young as myself calling for the Reaper, and I told him no more about his growing reputation back in England." Corfield cleared his throat. "Captain, I must tell you…"

FitzRoy steeled himself. "Yes?"

"He could very well die before the week is out."

"This is what the doctor said?"

"He did, but he didn't have to. You can see it in Charles himself."

"Can nothing save him?"

"Nothing but Providence, I believe," Corfield said. "At least he is as comfortable as possible."

FitzRoy very nearly muttered *Blast comfort!* but again checked his rebellious tongue, instead standing and placing his hat upon his head. "I thank you for your kindness to our mutual friend, sir."

"Will you not stay the night?"

"Many thanks to you, but as captain, I am required to sleep only aboard my ship," FitzRoy said, and allowed Corfield's summoned servant to lead him to the door. "You will send word if his condition takes a turn for... if there is a change?"

"Of course. You will be the first to know after myself."

They shook hands and bowed. FitzRoy left the house and began the short walk down to where the *Beagle* was docked, a plan forming in his mind to save his dearest friend. Upon reaching the ship and being received aboard by the few crew members on the top deck, he called over his coxswain and said, "Mister Bennett, I will be in my quarters. Unless war breaks out anew with France—no, even then—I am *not* to be disturbed."

ଓଃ ଓଃ ଓଃ

FitzRoy shut the door and immediately fell to his knees, his hands clasped and his eyes tightly shut, and spoke out loud: "Most powerful and glorious Lord God, at whose command the winds blow..." He could hear the words, was sure of their order—he read them to the crew every week—but on this occasion could not allow a syllable out of its rightful place. He leaned, still on his knees, to remove his *Book of Common Prayer* from its shelf and place it, opened to the usual page, on the edge of his writing desk.

"Lord, I know there must be a better prayer. I—I confess I have not studied your Book as I should..." He amazed himself by heaving in a sob and shedding a tear, which raced down his cheek. "But please hear me..." And he began again, his eyes clenched and his fingers intertwined, stopping after every score of words to look and make sure he was praying correctly:

> *Most powerful and glorious Lord God, at whose command the winds blow, and lift up the waves of the sea, and who stillest the rage thereof... We thy creatures—ah, we thy creatures...*

He leaned to squint at the page, then quickly resumed his position.

> *but miserable* sinners, *do in this our great distress cry unto thee for help: Save, Lord, or else we will perish... Or else we perish. We confess, when we have been safe, and seen all things quiet about us, we have forgot thee our God, and... and refused to hearken to the still voice of thy word, and to obey thy commandments: But now we see, how terrible thou art in all thy works of wonder; the great God to be feared above all: And therefore we love...*

Again he snuck a quick glance at the book.

> *... we* adore *thy Divine Majesty, acknowledging thy power, and imploring thy goodness. Help, Lord, and save us for thy mercy's sake in Jesus Christ thy Son, our Lord.* Amen.

Now, strengthened by hearing the words as he himself spoke them, he could see them on the page, in his mind, even with his eyes closed, and began a new prayer without once looking at the prayer book:

Most glorious and gracious Lord God, who dwellest in heaven, but beholdest all things below: Look down, we beseech thee, and hear us, calling out of the depth of misery, and out of the jaws of this death, which is ready now to swallow us up: Save, Lord, or else we perish. The living, the living shalt praise thee. O send thy word of command to rebuke the raging winds, and the roaring sea; that we, being delivered from this distress, may live to serve thee, and to glorify thy Name all the days of our life. Hear, Lord, and save us, for the infinite merits of our blessed Savior, thy Son, our Lord Jesus Christ. Amen.

This second sailor's prayer finished, FitzRoy's eyes popped open as he searched his mind for another prayer he knew by heart—one that would help Darwin defeat the death inside him—and finally it came. He shut his eyes again and began immediately, not worrying about a word here or there, but speaking, *shouting*, with full force and conviction to make certain that God should hear him:

Most powerful and glorious Lord God! The Lord of hosts that rulest and commandest all things!

FitzRoy gasped for air, sobs ripping the breath from his lungs—and leapt to the end of the prayer—

Make it appear that thou art our Savior and mighty Deliverer, through Jesus Christ our Lord! Amen. Amen!
Lord, please spare your servant, my brother, Charles Darwin! *Amen!*

Although he said not another word for the next four bells, FitzRoy remained on his knees with his hands wrapped together, his eyes closed and leaking tears as he promised everything he had, anything he would ever have, to the God he had so long neglected, if only He would answer this single prayer.

ଔ   ଔ   ଔ

The ship was as quiet as a grave, most of the crew being ashore and Bennett having relayed the captain's words to all who remained on board. So when FitzRoy heard the shifting sound of paper dashed under his cabin door, it may as well have been an explosion for how it pulled his attention back into the world of men.

He turned on his knees and picked up the envelope, which showed the seal of Richard Corfield of Valparaiso. Quickly opening the letter without the aid of a dagger, FitzRoy read the single, hastily scrawled line:

The fever has broken.

Vesalius

In this world, individuals cannot be distinguished by their outward appearance; humans are as similar to one another as penguins.

Their voices are all alike, as are their mannerisms and postures. Men and women mate by instinct, their ability to distinguish the opposite sex owing to nothing either party can put a finger on. All surface evidence points to a world of utter monotony.

But that is only the surface evidence. A scratched finger, a gouged eye, a weeping rash—all give rise to particularity, releasing the sufferer from anonymity, for everyone is different on the inside here, every single person has a distinct chemistry, and even the smallest amount of the inner workings made visible is enough to declare a unique identity to the rest of the world.

A razor slice, exposing the muscle beneath the skin, unleashes the essence of the man within like a mist of perfume. A broken bone, piercing into visibility, brings forth one's claims of individuality, something that can be sensed by everyone who comes into contact with the victim.

This is a world where the terribly wounded, spurred by the need to be seen, to be heard—to be *known*—are the celebrities. Their blood is their autograph; their bones their cathedrals; their beating hearts their symphonies.

Children are conceived through the essences contained in sperm, reaching into the womb and combining with the essences of the egg. At birth, children are scratched so that they can be named.

In time, people greet one another by spitting, or vomiting, or breaking wind, anything that releases their essences into the atmosphere. Blood and infection are everywhere; it is a world of death. To be known is to be doomed; everyone is aware of this fact and yet everyone seeks to bleed, so that others may know of their existence.

It is a world of skeletons, a world of peeled skin and hanging tongues. The more grotesque the injury, the more famous the individual, and the shorter his remaining life as he is exposed to decay and putrefaction, to the world of others.

However, one man does not cut himself, or spit, or fart around others. He keeps his skin as intact as at the moment he was born. His mother did not want him scraped, and so he has no name. He does not open himself, and so it is as if he has no face; he cannot be recognized by any streaming essences. He is a man alone in this world of screaming celebrity, of oozing identity, and he treasures this anonymity.

But in time, as the famous die and their slashed and broken contenders take their places in the public eye, there is no one else who has chosen to remain anonymous, who has kept his body in one piece, who has not exposed himself to the essences of other bodies. When this is noticed, he is no longer anonymous—but he is mysterious, and the bloodied come to see him, follow him, ask him questions about the nature of his existence, demand that he defend his decision to be the only person who is no one, and thus the only person remaining who is someone apart.

He runs from the living dead, the putrescent anatomies that scream for his name, that he must have a name and they must know it, and hides from them, his only shelter being that they cannot smell him, cannot sense his essence.

It does not last for long. The ambulant corpses drag their broken bodies, never sleeping, until he must come out for food or die himself. When they see him, they shriek and give chase, the bloody multitudes rushing up and surrounding him.

Too horrified even to scream, the anonymous celebrity pushes at the crowd, making himself a small circle in the gore, then reaches in his pocket for a razor and in one quick move slashes his own throat. A fountain gushes from his jugular, soaking those nearest him in even more blood. His essence spills out with it, and the scent of it wafts over the mob like woodsmoke.

They understand who he is now, an individual like them, another face in the crowd, a nobody. After a minute or two, as he falls to the ground, spurting the last of his blood, they can no longer see him, they no longer *want* to see him, this one who rejected individuality, rejected fame, rejected it when all those around him flayed themselves alive just to taste it for a moment.

Antemeridian

At the rear of the formation I fly, flapping my black wings in time to catch the updraft of my brother in front of me, easing my burden of flight.

Why don't we ever look down? What does the Earth look like from such a height? Our ten members make half a *V*; if I looked any way but straight ahead I could see right up the line at—

My brother all the way in front falls off the lead of the line, holding his wings still and coasting back behind me. Now my flapping provides him with extra lift as the brother in front of me provides me.

Is it cold up here? Do my feathers provide the proper insulation? Surely they do, else my species would travel in a different way, or to a different place, something more suited to our bodily form.

Or maybe our bodies changed in form when we started flying like this, flying to wherever we are going. Do I have a picture of it in my mind? Will I simply recognize it when we get there? The lead brother falls to the back again, and a sister now leads the way. What does the leader know? Does she know where we are going? Does she know when we are hungry?

After a couple of miles she too falls to the rear, and now I fly in the middle of the formation.

When did we start doing this? Whose idea was it to save energy by keeping a position to help with lift? What vote was taken to inspire us to change our leader every so often, to share the burden of being lead bird, the one who receives no extra lift, but only provides it?

There are just two in front of me now. I imagine I can see the horizon stretching across my field of vision, the way the ocean looks when viewed from the cliffs by the sea.

I am next. My sister exerts herself against the cutting wind, giving me the gift of ease, which I provide to the brother behind me. We are beauty, we are elegance in motion, we are the logical outcome of our needs and situation—

Now my sister falls off, out of my ken, and I am alone. I see only sky and green earth as I push my wings against the air. Where have they all gone? Where are my brothers and sisters? I don't know where I am going!

I have lost my family, the ones who led me on and kept me aloft. I let out a cry of anguish and exhaustion, and give up trying. I let my wings go slack and drift, drift and let a line of birds pass.

My family. I am swept up by their draft, and join them.

At the rear of the formation I fly, flapping my black wings in time to catch the updraft of my brother in front of me, easing my burden of flight.

Charles Island, Galapagos, 1835

Mister Lawson did not meet many new people as Vice-Governor of the tiny settlement on these tiny islands. Two hundred people he knew on a regular basis, two hundred Christians to be sure, but occupied with the meanest tasks of survival and not able to dine with him at his fine house on Charles Island, or not interested in doing so. It was a busy, but rather lonely, existence. It was for this reason that when he happened upon them during his visit to a whaling vessel— no gentlemen aboard, unfortunately, no one at all to talk to— it seemed like Providence itself.

For here at his island was the famous Captain FitzRoy— direct descendant of Charles II, nephew of Viscount Castlereagh, unfortunately a suicide, which precluded mention of his name at the table, but still! And the captain's particular friend, Mister Darwin, a naturalist, or perhaps a geologist. Keen minds, both! Lawson spent the day henpecking his servants, following them around in a state of agitated happiness, waiting for his guests to finish their business and finally, *finally* arrive for dinner.

The steward had no sooner announced "Captain FitzRoy and Mister Darwin, sir," than Lawson had whisked them into the sitting room and fastened their hands around tumblers of whiskey. "A pleasure to have you here, gentlemen, a pleasure!" Lawson said, catching his breath and taking a seat in the wicker chair across from theirs. "How do you find our bit of England this side of the world?"

"It is rather dry, isn't it?" FitzRoy said.

Lawson laughed heartily. "Indeed it is, sir! When the whalers stop here for provisions, I always wonder if they should not pay us with some of their water!"

FitzRoy and Darwin chuckled along with him, sharing a bemused glance.

"The volcanic soil must be good for lizards," Darwin said. "I would say they are the main animal I saw on the trip inland."

"Oh, yes, yes, we are very proud of our lizards here. They warm themselves all the day long on the black rock." Lawson shifted his eyes between his two guests. "But we have quite a variety of fauna here. Tortoises everywhere! The ones who live closer to the shore, they like it dry—but get their moisture from chewing the island's succulent cactus."

Darwin sat forward. This bit obviously had his interest, so Lawson continued, "How do they know to do that, I wonder, eh? The tortoises that live a thousand feet up, near the settlement here, they don't touch the cactus. They drink from puddles of fresh water left by the rain."

"There are no such puddles near the ocean?" FitzRoy said.

Darwin moved to answer him but Lawson jumped in: "Oh, no, Captain—an amazing feature of our black rock: It's as porous as a sponge, and just as good at sucking up any water that touches it. Amazing anything lives here at all, really."

Darwin did not seem nonplussed at being interrupted by their host, at which Lawson was relieved. "I do apologize,

Mister Darwin. I don't get to share my small store of geological knowledge very often out here."

"No problem, I assure you. The captain hears quite enough of my voice, and I doubt he minds hearing his lessons—always unasked-for and frequently unwanted, I'm sure—conveyed to him at least by a fresh one," Darwin said, and they laughed at the self-deprecation.

"Mister Darwin is entirely unfair to himself and to me," FitzRoy said, his thin lips curled over his teeth in a grin. "Why, only this morning the good man was lecturing me on how Jesus Himself couldn't *literally* have turned water into wine."

Lawson froze. Was this sea-captain bringing up religious disagreements in pre-prandial conversation? Not even the son of a whaler, who would have to be scrubbed down and disguised as a gentleman even to enter this room, would have made such a *faux pas*, insulting his companion in front of their host! "My dear Captain—"

But the companion, this odd young man with the thinning hair on top and the thick beard below, simply *laughed* at the affront. "Oh, no—I am not to be crucified for taking the wrong side of *this* argument, Robert! You play the Deist with me one day and Theist the next! I know not how to agree with you or, indeed, to disagree."

This was spoken with great jocularity, and the captain responded in kind. "But Charles, if a man can die and be reborn, then surely he can change one liquid chemical to another—it should be, as you always rush to tell me, trivial!"

"You put the cart before the horse," Darwin replied, "and have Him wreaking miraculous effects that precede the cause of these abilities—His Resurrection."

"Would you have Jesus prove His divinity before quenching the people's thirst?" FitzRoy was smiling as widely as ever as he applied his kill-shot: "Must He apply to your office with evidence before receiving His certificate?"

But Darwin was unfazed, and, almost laughing again, said, "If they were merely thirsty, the water would suffice. No need to get the people drunk and believing they are seeing miracles instead of simply a great man doing good works."

Lawson watched the volleys rebound between his guests, unable to get in a word as they played their odd verbal game. "Gentlemen, I don't—"

"When did you become such a literalist, anyway, Robert? You have always been devout, I don't deny it, but I remember a time when you had sport with me for quoting Scripture at the crew in support of my moral points."

For the first time, the captain's smile drooped, and the play between them sagged. "I regret that," he said. "Since that time, I have had... an *experience*."

Darwin glanced at Lawson, who knew not what to say, even now that there was a silence. "I assume this would not be the time to share the details of this experience."

FitzRoy now looked at Lawson as well, and the Vice-Governor wished that once, just one time, he could have guests, interesting guests, visit Charles Island who hadn't been driven utterly mad by the trip around the Horn. Lawson sighed, then stiffened to a proper posture and said, "I do not wish to be an impediment to understanding between friends."

"Not at all," FitzRoy said. "It is only this: I prayed with my whole heart for... for something of great value. The Lord in His infinite goodness granted my request, and His price was that I forever take Him at His word, absolutely. If His Book says that Jesus turned water to wine, then I believe Him—I owe Him my complete surrender and obsequity, and as a gentleman I always pay my debts. I will tell you no more, but it is a small price for such a treasure as I received, I assure you."

Darwin marveled at FitzRoy and said, his voice seeming to come from far away, "Turning water into wine is nothing compared to this, turning a naturalizing Deist into a proselytizing Theist."

"It is a miracle," FitzRoy said, and put his hand on his friend's shoulder, "and one that you will come to in time as well. If you ever are in real need, all you must do is appeal to our Lord, pray to Him with a pure heart. And He will provide."

Darwin moved to say something, no doubt to contradict his captain, but just then the doors opened and the steward announced it was time to move into the dining room. Very softly, Lawson gave *his* thanks to God.

ප   ප   ප

By the time they had finished with soup and started on the main course, Lawson noted with relief, the earlier conversation had been left in the sitting room and the food had claimed the center of attention.

"By my word, this is truly capital chicken," Darwin said to Lawson, savoring his latest bite. At the Vice-Governor's smile, he added self-consciously, "Have I said something amusing?"

"Not at all," Lawson said. "I smile because that is exactly the reaction I had upon first being served the meat of *Testudo nigra*."

"This is *tortoise?*" Darwin wondered at the room, and his chewing slowed as he tried to detect something of the sea in the taste. "Robert, have you ever tasted such tender flesh, outside of pen-raised pork?"

"I certainly have not," the captain allowed, "and I have eaten turtle many times."

Lawson felt as chuff as cheese. "Please allow me the impudence of correcting your way of thinking, my good Captain—this is a James Island tortoise, no web-footed turtle. It takes eight men to lift one of these magnificent creatures, and two men alone are not enough to turn one of them onto its back. All that size—two hundred pounds of meat!—and it is the most tender eating of any tortoise of the Galapagos."

"I don't follow you," Darwin said. "Certainly these Islands' tortoises all would taste the same?"

"I would agree if I had not been here five years," Lawson answered, and put down his fork in anticipation of being able to tell his guest—his learned, articulate guest—something new. "But you can quite tell which of our islands a particular tortoise hails from simply by the patterns on its shell. And the shape of the shells—the animals from here and from Hood Island have them extra thick in front, turned up like a Spanish saddle. On James Island they're blacker and rounder—and, as I say, are better eating than any other."

"But these islands are in sight of one another," Darwin said. "This much diversity is not to be found in the whole of the South American continent!"

"The tortoises are hardly alone in their plenitude of difference. Our birds—finches, I believe—have unique faces on each island, and there are many other interesting species besides."

"Might make for some good shooting, Charles," FitzRoy said. "Send some specimens back to Reverend Henslow, see what he makes of them."

"Perhaps I will. Although a finch is a finch, I believe." Darwin suddenly shuddered, the color draining from his face.

"My word, man! Are you quite all right?" Lawson cried, rising from his seat in alarm.

But Darwin held up a hand to signal him to sit back down. "It is a touch of the illness I acquired in South America. Sudden chills, wracking pains... I have no doubt but that I will have a fever tonight."

"Is there nothing that can be done for it? No physic you can take?"

The color returning to Darwin's face, he turned to Fitz-Roy and said, "I daresay I remember this sickness once bringing me to knock on death's very door! These attacks are merely very... unpleasant." Darwin smiled and took another bite of the James tortoise. "This meal, on the other hand... Perhaps I *should* take some notes on the animals here, see if I can't contrive a cookery-book, as the Americans call it."

"It would sell out in a day," Lawson said with cheer.

FitzRoy added, "The whaleboat is yours for the asking, Charles."

"I suppose it would be a waste not to see this variety, this practical infinitude of creatures you describe," Darwin said. "At the very least, a trip among the islands should prove diverting, even if nothing of scientific value comes of it."

Leibniz

The naturalist balances atop the giant tortoise as the beast makes its way across the beach, rocking like a ship's hammock in the swells. The sky is in gorgeous uproar, purple and black clouds chasing white gulls which swoop and rise.

"This is the best of all possible worlds," the tortoise says, slowly. It is the size of a post-chaise and yet grows. "It is a world of infinite variety and plenitude."

The naturalist scoffs good-naturedly. "Infinity is not provable; it cannot be quantified or qualified and thus should have no place in the vocabulary of an educated amphibian."

The tortoise eases them off the sand and into the water, where it floats like a bubble on a stream. The naturalist can see its legs gently oaring as they move out into the sea. Its head is underwater, but he can still clearly understand the reptile's words: "Our finite experience of eternity gives us no reason to doubt nature's unlimited goodness and plenitude."

"These are only words, friend Tortoise; I see no evidence for this plenitude."

The tortoise loops his head up out of the water and fixes the naturalist with a smile of incredulity. "You see no evidence? The variety of the Galapagos is not evidence enough for you to accept the goodness and infinite variety of the universe?"

"I have seen a great deal of variety, certainly—but not infinity."

The tortoise's head ducks back under the water, bubbles of effortful breath rising from its nostrils. The naturalist totters and grasps for purchase as his companion rises from the water, legs outstretched into wings, its head cutting the air as they fly.

"I will show you infinity, my dear philosopher." The tortoise takes them up, up, into the furious sky, through the black clouds full of lightning, above them into the blue atmosphere, above that into the blackness of the æther, above that into the gossamer fog of the galaxy.

"Are we going to Heaven?" the naturalist asks, breathing in the cool vapors of space. "What else could be so high?"

"Don't be naïve." The tortoise whirls and brings them around another sun, this one tinged with blue instead of suffused with yellow. Around this sun spins an orb much like Earth, only with two moons, and an ocean of green. "Look down there," the tortoise tells him, and leans to one side as they fly near the planet. "Look at the plenitude, and dare to tell me it is less than infinite."

The naturalist peers down and watches unicorns frolicking with centaurs; as soon as his mind has taken this in, the tortoise shuttles them to another solar system. Here, Greek medusae fight with jelly-bulls. Another leap through the æther; another world, this one with clouds of vaporous beings, without color or form but creating a wake visible to the eye, drifting past creatures formed entirely of rock.

"Are you not diverted?" the tortoise says. "There is no kind of creature which does not live on some world in this perfect universe of plenty."

The naturalist wishes he could shoot and take specimens back to the waking world, but how does one bag and dissect a being made of vapor? He smiles at the thought, but the smile fades as he looks up once again into the luminous powder of the Milky Way. "Let us go home now, friend Tortoise; I have seen enough to fill journals for the rest of my days."

The great animal fills its lungs with æther and dives back into the void, racing by planet after planet in their infinite variety. Finally they come to a small, blue world and plunge through the atmosphere, down to the very tip of a large continent, not to the island of the Galapagos from whence they came, but to Terra del Fuego. On the beach he can see the Fuegians, running and stealing and defecating and copulating, barely the same species as Man; not far from them, he can see himself, his wide-brimmed hat shading his face as he reaches after a crab. Looking down onto the deck of the *Beagle*'s whale boat, he can see the captain, cap upon his head, discussing some order of business with his coxswain.

But as the tortoise banks to bring them to a landing in the shallows, the naturalist spies a curiosity—it is his own face under the captain's cap! Instinctively he turns to take in the man on the beach and sees the face of his captain on the man collecting specimens, long brown beard and all.

"There is some mistake," he says to the tortoise as they glide in towards the shore. "The naturalist creature and the sea-captain creature are reversed in this world."

The tortoise takes in the sight and snorts, his shell reverberating with amusement. "So they are! My apologies, dear man. With this plenitude of worlds, it is easy to mistake one Earth for another that would be its twin but for one accident of circumstance."

They lift up and off once again, out into space, to another blue world, to the tip of the large continent, to this planet's

Terra del Fuego. As they touch down on the water, the naturalist instantly sees that something is terribly wrong—the naturalist on the shore and the captain on the ship are both brown of skin and long of hair, while the near-animals that caper upon the beach have the faces of the naturalist, the captain, the swain, the bosun, all of the men he has traveled with this many a year! They frolic as the Fuegians do, completely naked, while the savages in white men's clothes execute their duties with solemnity.

"What mockery of a world is this? This cannot be… can it?"

"*Every* configuration of life exists in our world of infinite plenitude. For there to be even one missing would be a stain on its ultimate goodness, since the best world is one which includes everything." It pauses, turning and paddling away from the shore. "I seem to have simply lost my heading a bit."

"I want to return to my world, please, friend Tortoise."

"Yes, of course," it says, and they lift off again, sail through the heavens again to another blue world and coast towards the island at the… the very… tip…

But here there is no island at the tip of South America. There is no Terra del Fuego, no *Beagle*, no naturalist and his captain.

"We must try again!" the naturalist shouts, leaving decorum behind. "We—how many Earths *are* there?"

"An infinity," the tortoise says in a voice that sounds drained of blood. "There are an infinity of blue Earths within the infinity of all Earths."

"All Earths? What madness is this?"

"Green Earths, red Earths, Earths without color, Earths without life. The infinity of Earths is but one infinity within the infinity of all worlds." He sighs and dips his head in the water to cool off, or to hide, before lifting it again and saying blankly, "I am tired. We will never find your exact Earth again."

The naturalist blanches. "Then—then please take me to the England of *this* Earth, whatever it is. To Cambridge."

Defeated, the tortoise nods and rises just over the water, skimming the surface at such a speed that the sun moves south in the sky and England is below them in a matter of minutes. The naturalist's clothes are made wet, then torn, then stripped away entirely by the rushing wind. The tortoise collapses on the green quad of Queen's College, and gasps for breath, exhausted, and dies. The naturalist climbs down, naked and panting, and cries, partly with sadness at the loss of his friend, partly with the joy of being home.

But this is not home.

Classes let out and from the hallowed halls, over marble steps and through leafy paths—paths in another world walked by Isaac Newton—come the savages, the Fuegians, their brown skin and hairy hands poking out from their dress shirts and neckties, nothing but savages bent over and barking at one another, nothing but savages everywhere. As they notice his pale skin and upright posture, the students and professors smile with curiosity, and come to take him away, to study and to pity him, this accident of circumstance.

Antemeridian

When nothing is left of the sinking ship that one can hold on to, it does not take long for one, if he is not a swimmer, to take his last breath and slip under the salty waves for the last time. He falls and falls deeper into the green, then the blue, then the purple, then the black, all the time holding his breath, holding it to what end, to what purpose? It is only so he can feel the crushing pressure of the water against his sides, so when he finally must release his breath he can feel the brine forced inside him, so that even his thinking of himself objectively to stave off panic fails and I thrash—he thrashes—against the entire ocean, begging for breath, coughing water and breathing in water that sets my lungs afire and slowly, slowly, slowly makes me heavy as an anchor and pulls me down to where I fight no more.

The *Beagle*, off New South Wales, 1836

Darwin's fevers had become more common, almost nightly now, his gut more churning, his muscles more cramping than ever. He put on a brave face for the captain and the crew, but after his 130-mile trek inland to Bathurst, during which he kept his spirits up by spotting and bagging many exotic creatures, he could not hide his desperate exhaustion from his loyal assistant.

What in the devil is wrong with me? he wondered for the thousandth time as Covington helped him into his hammock aboard ship. *Why do I remain alive, if I am to suffer this permanent sickness?*

"I don't rightly know, sir," Covington said, putting a blanket over him.

"What's that?"

"I say, I don't know why you're alive, sir, being so sick. But allow me to say I'm mighty gratified that you are."

"Kind of you," Darwin muttered. God help him—he was muttering his private thoughts out loud now, like an invalid given completely over to his malady. He almost drifted off, but started awake and called out, "Wake me for tea, won't you?"

"Of course, sir," his assistant said, sounding mildly surprised.

"I mean, I don't doubt I'll be wakened. It's only that——" Darwin paused, but then carried on——"please to make sure that the captain is not the one to wake me, nor his man Bennett, but only you."

Covington put a knuckle to his forehead, a private joke between them since Darwin was no officer, and closed the door behind him.

Darwin collapsed back onto his hammock, already dazed from the fever. If he could not keep his private thoughts to himself, he would have to leave the ship and arrange private transport back to England. The ideas in his head were things he was ready for no man alive to hear.

Suarez

In this world, the theists are right: Every individual creature is specifically fashioned by God.

There are no accidents of biological history, no fortuitous or unlucky effects of design. There has never been a plant or animal form that was not forged intentionally and specifically by the divine Hand. Biology in this world is a popular guessing game played for stakes by idle gentlemen speculating what God's reasons could be for creating this particular being or that. Over the centuries, since the beginning of the Renaissance, complex rules have been developed to keep the game fair and interesting.

Sea-lions are a favorite topic of biology clubs around Europe. Strong sea-lions are each created to keep the fish population under control; weak sea-lions, of which there are fewer, are each created to provide for the well-being of the cetaceous *Orcinus orca*, for whom the seals are a favorite meal. All are kept in precise proportions, God never making one more or one fewer than needed, and all growing to whatever proportions that best suit their role.

Unlike with Aristotle's *telos*, the species as a whole does not excite comment from those interested in biology; a species is simply a collection of like creatures, most fashioned for a similar, but not identical, purpose by God, a purpose that is filled by the entirety of that creature's very existence. Saying that a species is an actual entity is like saying that constellations are actual entities, rather than chance conglomerations of similar things in interesting patterns.

Beavers as a group build dams, but a particular beaver is born in the North American wilderness to die at a particular time, fall into the river, and distract a brown bear from eating a particular salmon, which then swims upstream towards its nesting place before leaping into the mouth of a different brown bear. This second bear was created specifically by God to knock down a particular tree in three years' time. Why the tree had to be knocked down is left to the arborists, an entirely separate group of theological entrepreneurs.

A schism divides the Shrewsbury Chapter of Biological Speculators, over the intent of God with respect to individual humans. It was all very well when God could be thought to create weaker and lesser forms of rabbits, or birds, or even dogs and horses; they became food for their predators when stronger specimens did not; but why would He specifically create diseased, stunted, suffering humans?

"We are prey for no animal, and so no reason for lesser humans can be discerned," says the President of the Chapter. "Therefore Man must be exempt from specific design and creation. God wants us to rely on our free will and moral choice to avoid disease, misfortune, small stature, and like conditions. A leper is a *moral* failure, not a biological one. God did not create him specifically in order to have another leper in the world."

"But where is the sport in that?" cries the opposition leader. "All creatures must be treated equally under the rules—otherwise how can the game be played? One cannot guess the reason for a particular man's birth if he decides his own reason through will and choice."

"Then Man must be put above other creatures in the ladder of existence—he is created in order to satisfy God, and that is reason enough!"

A chorus of boos and hisses from the opposition fills the Shrewsbury hall. "That is not science, sir. Without consistent rules for gambling and speculation, what you propose is anarchy, nothing but... *secularism!*"

This is the end of argument and the beginning of war. Science on the one side, touting reasonable explanations of the Special Creation of every creature on Earth, using these explanations to generate profit and intellectual diversion; and the Church on the other side, claiming that God is ineffable and His works are His alone to understand, using this mystery in the service of the less fortunate. The Church works for diseases to be cured, not simply for the existence of the diseased to be explained. Science works towards a communion with God through correctly surmising and supporting His goals, not for some progress here on Earth.

A few years after the schism, the Church bans gambling, a move that forever separates the two spheres of influence. The world should not depend on luck and superstition, as the scientists would have it; instead, sound principles of cause and effect are relied upon. Prayer is seen as useless in the face of a mysterious God who desires only to be worshipped, not understood, and so the Church abandons prayer as being a form of gambling as well.

The Church is, above all, relentlessly practical: Worship consists of improving the lot of Mankind through intellectual progress and technological innovation. Women are included in all ecclesiastical functions—research and development, design and implementation, even mathematics—since all hands are needed to remake the world, not just men's.

Incensed by the move, scientists adapt: No longer content as idle gentlemen, they instead become professionalized, using investigations of sacred books and myths to back up their claims of God's intent and to improve the accuracy of the odds used in biological gaming. To counter the Church's ban on gaming—science's most hallowed institution—scientists ban experimentation as "cheating," trying to "beat the odds" and subvert God's will. Women are kept subordinate to men, since it is wagered that this is why God made them physically smaller and weaker, why they suffer menstruation and bear children.

There is no such thing as an atheist in this world; there are only those who trust in God's reasoning for each Special Creation and focus on making the world a better place—that is, the Church, the secular—and those who feel the need to work out God's reasoning behind the actual functioning of each Creation and how He relates it to all other forms of life—that is, Science, the religious.

Antemeridian

"Your mother is waiting on you, Bobby."

"Mother is dead, sir; I remember that clearly."

"Go to her now, boy, and let me hear no more of your cheek."

"Where can I find her—at the graveyard?"

"Don't be dramatic. If she wants to see you, then she would be waiting in the garden, wouldn't she? Like always."

"In the garden. Yes, sir."

"And Bobby? Tell her there will be no dinner for the dead."

ಚಿ ಚಿ ಚಿ

Mother waiting her pale flesh peeling over cheekbone.

"It is good to see you again, Mummy. I thought you had gone already."

Mother's smile is floating kiss Mummy on worm-burrowed face.

"Why are you in the garden? Did you forget something?"

Bobby will come with Mummy down cold earth clutch hold her Mother is cold.

"But I'm not dead. I have many important things to do. The world is my oyster, Father says. I cannot leave dear Fanny and my daughters! What of the *Beagle* and the water cure?"

Mother's eye clenches heaves a tear from dryness empty sockets.

"I *do* love you, Mum! I will be in my grave soon enough; can you not wait an hour, a fortnight, a year or ten? I am fifty-seven years old, and I'll be thirteen next week, and I shall shoot a tern last year using an axe handle with the safety still on."

Mother shrieks on her feet DO NOT DIE! Chobert Rodwin Darles, you do not dare to die! The ground is cold and the worms are hungry! Mother's tongue a mass of moss grown to smother her.

 C3   C3   C3

I am awake. I lie abed, eyes closed and still sleeping, but my mind is awake.

Mother is here, in the room.

Go away. I am afraid. I am fading.

C3   C3   C3

"Did you tell her?"

"I'm sorry, Father… tell her what?"

"That there will be no dinner for the dead."

"I—I did not, sir. She frightened me and I forgot."

"Then she will be back."

The *Beagle*, at sea, 1836

"Mister Darwin for tea, sir," Bennett called into the captain's cabin a few hours later, whispering to the guest, "He's in a mischievous humor tonight, Mister Philos, sir."

Darwin had no time to react to the steward's comment, but knew exactly what was meant as soon as he saw FitzRoy sitting at the table, his hair combed forward over its receding border, his jacket on, complete with epaulets. Such a fancy state of dress could mean only one thing: In his own mind, FitzRoy had gained the upper hand in their ongoing argument.

"Charles! Come, take a seat. I understand you harbor a secret."

"What—I—"

FitzRoy's face betrayed his glee. "Ah, you're delirious with guilt! Confession is good for the soul, they say—let's get your secret off your chest."

Indeed at that moment Darwin's chest felt as if a great and icy weight had been placed upon it, freezing his feet to the floor and his face into a rictus that showed equal parts shock and dismay.

"Goodness, Darwin—I was only joking!" FitzRoy cried, and rushed to his friend's aid, helping him into the chair he had only a moment before taunted him with. "Are you quite all right, man?"

Darwin gulped a lungful of air. "Fine! Fine. I have to admit, your words took me by surprise. What is this 'secret' with which you torture me? I'm sure I don't know what you could mean."

Seeing that his companion was in fact well, FitzRoy regained his playful smile and retook his own seat on the other side of the table. "I think you *do* know, but it is only that you do not realize the import of the secret in question."

"Robert, I know you're having fun, but please to speak plainly, if you would. My head is in no condition for riddles."

"All right," FitzRoy said, his spirit not dimmed in the least, "I understand that last week, when you and Covington walked inland in Australia, you *personally* witnessed evidence that God undertook *two* Creations, as I have always maintained and you have always just as steadfastly refused to accept."

Now feeling he was in a game with an unusual card-sharper, Darwin took his time sifting through anything he might have seen on his trip inland—and that could have been reported without his knowledge—that could have given Fitz-Roy this impression. Almost immediately, it came to him, because Covington had marveled so long at the creature that even then his employer could have predicted he would blabber about it immediately upon coming aboard. Could have predicted it—but hadn't.

He closed his eyes and said flatly, "The platypus."

"Aye, the platypus!" FitzRoy gloated, and slapped his palm on the table. "Webbed feet on a furry mammal! One that lays eggs but suckles its young with milk! And two coats of fur, no less, on an animal with a duck's bill! It is prime proof that the Bible shows no contradictions—there were two Creations."

"Yes, yes, yes. One thousands of millions of years since, the one 'In the beginning'—which God destroyed first—and then a second six thousand years since, with Adam and Eve and the Garden of Eden and so on. What of it, my friend?"

"I don't care for your dismissive tone—this explanation perfectly answers the geologic record, defending the Bible against atheism and naturalism."

"Not so long ago you considered *yourself* quite the naturalist, I recall."

"In terms of honoring God's work, I still do, Charles. The Lord is to be seen in nature—not to be pushed aside because of it." FitzRoy's smile was gone. "I worry about your soul, my friend."

"My *soul?* Am I so godless as all that, simply because I say—" He brought himself up short, hoping the horror that had seized him was not revealed by his countenance.

"Because you say...?" FitzRoy waited. "Because you say what you have said at this very table—that God sent the universe a-spinning and then sat back, pipe in hand, doing no more in the lives of His creatures?"

"Yes, of course—yes, exactly that." Darwin breathed out, thankful for FitzRoy's habit of demeaning opinions he did not also hold. "But to the point: What has this to do with my platypus? How is that perplexing creature a sign of two acts of Creation?"

FitzRoy had been smiling again, but now any trace of triumph melted away as he said in a manner that showed he could hardly believe Darwin had asked the question, "I... I say this, dear Philos, because... it is what you yourself said upon seeing the animal. Covington reported to his messmates that he heard you with his own ears, muttering exactly those words!"

A wave of relief washed over Darwin. "Ah, that silly Covington, bless him—he misheard me in his fascination with the creature, as well as the fact that I intended the words for no one other than myself. I assure you, what I actually said is in quite the opposite sense to what he reported."

"I fail to see how that could be. You had a revelation from the workings of God, and now you shy from—"

"Robert, *Robert*, please," Darwin said, and steeled himself against any spray of Hot Coffee. "I did say the words Covington ascribes to me, with one exception: I said 'two *Creators*,' not 'two Creations.'"

"Two Creators? I don't even understand what such a phrase could mean."

"It means, my dear, that the platypus, with its bizarre collection of features, seemed to me more like a confused product of two competing Creators than the purposeful work of one."

The color rose in FitzRoy's cheeks, as it had so many times during their heated discussions, especially since his illness at Valparaiso. The captain stood.

"Robert, please don't upset yourself over a careless remark muttered in—"

"No, it's not that. We have but a few months remaining in our voyage. Let us enjoy them as friends."

"Absolutely," Darwin said with relief. But FitzRoy did not sit down.

"And in the interest of that friendship, please dine here in my cabin, without me. I will tell Bennett to bring mine to me on deck. Good day to you, sir."

Darwin didn't try to say anything as FitzRoy swept from the room. They might as well have been of two Creators now, for all their worlds would overlap once they reached the shores of England again, FitzRoy high and mighty in his world of certainty, Darwin low and feeble in his world of doubt.

He remained in the cabin as ordered and took his tea, the great secret his only companion until the illness made its inevitable return.

William of Occam

In this world, the famous principle holds: *entia sunt multi-plicanda praeter necessitatem* ("entities should be multiplied beyond need"). Here, the more unnecessarily complex an idea, the closer it is considered to absolute Truth.

Therefore, members of scientific societies compete to produce the most labyrinthine theories for even the seemingly simplest natural occurrences. Monstrous professional journals dedicate hundreds of pages to a single formulation of a single change to a single extant theory. Magical or chimærical influences on the weather are duly proposed and argued about; traces of long-ago traumas are cited as causal in house fires; invisible, wholly undetectable faeries are included in the explanation of nonrepetition in the shapes of snowflakes.

A fresh redundancy introduced into a theoretical framework thought to be optimally complicated can result in fame, funding, an endowed chair of natural philosophy. The insertion of a causal loop—that is, infinite redundancy—into a theory is the kind of discovery that young philosophers dream about, as close to knowing the mind of God to which a human being can aspire. God Himself is seen as the highest Truth in redundancy and complexity, a Being with an identical pres-

ence everywhere but too complicated to be fully compre-
hended anywhere, an impenetrable diamond.

This is the status quo for many years, before a young clergyman just out of seminary realizes that an even greater Truth
than *one* perfectly redundant and complicated God would be
two of them. Or more—an infinity of Gods. Not as the Hindoos would have it—three hundred million distinct deities
with distinct roles and personalities—but instead an infinity of
divine beings identical in every way. There would be no purpose to such redundancy, since God's qualities are absolute;
one million omnipotent Gods would be no more powerful
than a single omnipotent God; one thousand million omni-
scient Gods would know nothing that one would not know.

And since every point in space would already be filled with
even one perfect God, any naturalist trying to explain how an
infinity of them could exist at the same points would have to
perform some complicated logical contortions indeed. It was
not a step in the direction of ultimate Truth—it was an auda-
cious *leap*.

Announcing his discovery to a church packed with breathless scientists and theologians from around Europe, the young
clergyman's very first question comes from a rumpled stranger
in the back, his chest-length beard a tangled bush of white. "If
God is indeed in every point in space, He has created every
one of us to share that space with Him," the stranger croaks.
"Even more so if there are infinite Gods. That's why we all
exist. That's *how* we all exist. Simple, yes?"

The clergyman nods guardedly. The audience in the pews
have never seen this man, don't know what society or church
he is with, and so say nothing. But the reviled word—"simple"—hangs in the air.

The stranger nods as well. "And we have all been created but once, every creature and every *kind* of creature. The very model of theoretical thrift, wouldn't you agree?"

He waits for a new nod from the clergyman, but when none comes, the stranger continues anyway. "But how much more complicated, how much more redundant—how much closer to Truth!—would be the explanation for our existence if there were no God at all."

Frightened and excited rumbling spreads through the sanctuary.

"Gentlemen, I tell you it would be *immensely* complicated! How did life arise, how did Man arise, without the simple inspiration of God, without the touch of His finger to our ancestor of inanimate clay? Without that, it must be random matter giving rise spontaneously to lower life, then ascending of some mysterious power to higher forms, and finally to something as wondrous as Mankind? Any accounting for that must be a million million times more complicated, more difficult to grasp than any supernatural explanation!"

"That's very well, sir, but what of redundancy?" counters the young clergyman. "A solid theory must—"

"Redundancy? If you want redundancy, then I give you a new act of creation with every single birth of every single human, every animal, every bird, fish, and insect that has ever walked, swum, or flown! With no God to say simply, 'Life is good,' every act by every creature at every point in time is the *same* effort, sir! Every success the same as every other success—new life—and every failure the same as every other failure—extinction of that line of descent. *Perfect* redundancy, my good man."

The room is silent now; the wan clergyman grips the pulpit to keep himself standing. All watch as the stranger collects his hat and his walking stick and slowly walks up the aisle and out of the church. As the giant doors close behind him, the assembly of theologians and scientists gaze upon one another in disbelief.

"Who was that?" one of them asks.

"Simple in his ideas, elegant in his explanations, the enemy of Truth," the clergyman says. "That was the Devil."

Antemeridian

dust sperm egg embryo fœtus baby child man pain bend
corpse rot dust sperm egg embryo fœtus baby child corpse rot
dust sperm dust sperm egg embryo blood dust sperm egg embryo fetus baby child woman birth pain bend corpse rot dust
bacterium insect earthworm fish frog lizard bird mouse rat
cat dog horse elephant monkey chimpanzee sperm egg embryo fœtus baby child woman man God
dust sperm egg embryo fœtus baby child God man
God pain joy pain corpse dust man

London, 1837

On Marlborough Street, in the rooms he had let for Syms Covington and himself, Darwin's head lay on his desk, in a tiny depression he had dug out from the mountains of books and papers, diaries and sketchbooks. Directly under his left temple was a letter from Gould at the London Zoo Museum, telling him that the many birds he brought back from the Galapagos were all varieties of finch, with the principle difference being the structure of their beaks. Reading this, he once again could see only evidence that a new explanation of speciation was needed, because miraculous design or other divine causes could no longer pretend to scientifically explain it, and this gave him a new attack in his gut. Even if he accepted the transmutation of species—professional suicide, but this way hypothetical—he still had no idea by what mechanism this was to be achieved, and without that his ideas were no more scientific than William Paley's. He would keep his head down until he could think of a solution, like the Buddha of the Asiatics, sitting under his tree until he achieved salvation.

With his line of sight thus blocked by the piled materials recording the voyage of the *Beagle*, he could only hear the door squeak on its old-fashioned hinges, followed by the equally squeaky voice of Covington:

"Dead already today, sir?"

"It is impolite to disturb the recently departed, Syms."

"Begging your pardon, then. But I have news. An invitation, actually."

Darwin lifted his head. It still felt strange to him not to have his long brown beard, and his clean-shaven face now showed lines from the papers on which he had rested. "An invitation?" he said with great interest. "From Reverend Henslow? Has he heard from the Royal Society on my finds?"

"Um… no, sir. I mean, he hasn't sent word on it. Of course, he could have—"

"Then what is this invitation? What is the news? Has the publisher been asking for my book?" He chuckled, for the first time in several days, and gestured towards the piles of materials. "I'm only one man, and there is such a wealth of information here to be assimilated."

"Begging your pardon again, sir, but the news has to do with Captain FitzRoy."

Darwin groaned—silently, he hoped, but Covington's expression showed otherwise—and put his head back on the desk. "Go on, then."

Covington pulled a large envelope from his satchel and handed it to his employer. It bore FitzRoy's seal and was addressed to Darwin. "I ran into Mister Bennett when I was picking up the post. He was just putting a stamp on this when he noticed me, and asked if I could instead present to you personally. He said the Captain is quite excited to have you there."

Now Darwin let out a sigh to accompany his earlier groan. "What is it this time? Another public announcement of thanks made by Parliament? Another commendation from the Admiralty?" He looked to Covington, who could not properly say anything, but Darwin felt he could read his assistant's mind. "I—I am very happy for our dear Captain, who is also my particular friend, you may remember. I am very happy for him, Syms."

"Of course you are, sir. And you've been handsomely received by the naturalists, the geologists and... all them, right? Each of you is famous in your own... em—*sphere of influence*, as they say."

Darwin nodded without hesitation. So what if his sphere was limited to rock collectors and Cambridge professors, while FitzRoy's encompassed all of higher society and the greater scientific community? This was the captain's rightful place, a gentleman among gentlemen, and he had toiled for five hard years to produce the surveys for which he was being lauded. Darwin felt a wave of shame at his jealousy. He was sure that once his journal of the *Beagle*'s voyage was complete and published, he would have his day in the sun... even if it was at a less direct exposure than the one FitzRoy now enjoyed.

"If I may—please to open the envelope, sir. I am fair to choked with curiosity about our Captain's latest announcement."

"As am I," Darwin said brightly, and used his dagger. Inside the large envelope were two smaller envelopes—one addressed with FitzRoy's unmistakable handwriting, and one in the hand of a woman.

"Bennett *did* save himself some post!" Covington said, and they laughed.

Darwin opened the letter from FitzRoy first, and shut his eyes against the surge of unchristian envy that erupted from his soul.

"Is everything all right with the Captain, sir?"

"Quite all right," Darwin forced himself to say. "He asks me to attend a reception at the Royal Geographic Society——"

"That's the place for you, indeed!"

"——where he will be presented, for his work on the *Beagle*, with the Society's gold medal. Their highest honor."

"Well," Covington said, his eyes pointed to the floor. "Good on him, eh?"

"Right. Of course. He deserves the honor greatly."

A silence filled the room, but Covington broke it finally by nodding at the second envelope and saying, "Any idea what that one might be?"

"Let us find out together." Darwin broke the seal on the second envelope and recognized it instantly for what it was. "My God."

"Mister Darwin, sir?"

"The Captain is getting married. We are invited to the wedding."

"*We?* Well, that's capital of him to include your humble servant…" Covington said with a smile, but a cloud soon covered his face. "Sir, pardon the cheek, but has the Captain ever mentioned knowing a special lady at home?"

Darwin had been thinking the same thing. "He has not."

"But we've been back not even three whole month."

"True." His lips twitched in amusement.

"My God," Covington said, then caught himself. "Eh—all I mean to say, sir, is—pardon my cheek once again, but… if the Captain surveyed coastlines as efficiently as he has London's eligible women, we would have been home two year ago."

Darwin shared a laugh with his assistant—his only companion in London—and set the invitations down. He would attend both of the celebrations, of course, and wear a genuine smile at both, but he was aware that he was watching his friend's life sail off from his own, reaching latitudes Darwin could only wonder at, while he remained stuck in the doldrums, wanting for any breath of wind.

The Hindoos

In this world, metempsychosis has been empirically proven.

After the death of one body, naturalists have demonstrated, the soul transmigrates into another newly born, this last being merely the latest in an uncountable series of separate corporeal existences. By performing a series of controlled experiments using finely calibrated balances and electrical dynamos, science has confirmed the Hindoos' ancient concept of reincarnation.

Using an ingenious algorithmic process developed by Dr. Mesmer himself, scientists are able to bring about a conscious awareness of individuals' former incarnations in the individuals themselves. From that point on, one's memory stretches back to earlier adulthood, to childhood, to infancy, and then to the end of one's previous incarnation, to earlier times in that life, then to the end of the life preceding that one, and so on, back thousands of years. After that, the memories become less and less distinct, until it fails altogether. But the physical theologians constantly experiment to refine the method and reach farther back.

Mesmerization is expensive, beyond the normal means of most townsmen, but the hunger for revelation forces even the poorest to sell and scrounge and steal in order to pay for a glimpse of who they have been, who they are, who they might still be.

It excites men, tortures them.

Each day at a certain time the baker watches the judge's wife walk by his shop window. She is an elegant woman, with a slim waist, long neck, smooth skin. Her head is covered, but the baker can see the curls of her midnight hair peeking out, and her servant's arms are often filled with packages, her own hands full of letters she reads and laughs about even as she passes.

For the hour before she appears at his window, the baker can scarcely feel his hands on the dough. Its blood drawn away, his face is white as flour. He has burned himself on the ovens many times, spinning to see her regal bearing when she comes into view a few minutes early. When she is late, all work ceases in his kitchen until she has finally made her appearance, passed by, and vanished once again. Days when she does not visit his street are gray and without mercy.

The baker has sold his business to an owner in another town so he could pay for the mesmerization. He now works for the profit of another, but it is all worth it if he can impress the judge's wife, make her see he is not just some baker. In fact, being a baker disgusts him when he thinks of how she must see him, covered in sugar and flakes of wheat, a vulgar working man.

But if only she could know what he was in his past lives! A general, a queen, a judge! (Also in other lives a starving infant, a convict, a whore, but there would be no cause to mention these.) He has been a wealthy landowner, a gladiator, a philosopher, a knight.

Emboldened by this information, the baker closes his shop at midday, having cleaned himself up and pinned a rose to the lapel of his only suit. Minutes later, the judge's wife comes around the corner. The baker is seized with excitement and anxiety, but his resolve remains firm: He will tell her who he is, who he has been, tell her at long last that he loves her.

She walks up, modestly not looking at him as befits someone of her status. But the baker cannot miss this opportunity and blurts, "Missus!"

She stops and fixes him with a curious glare. Finally her lips break into a smile and she says, "Mother? Mother!"

The baker is rendered speechless. "No, Missus, I—"

But he is interrupted now by the change in her expression, the corners of her mouth drawing down, her eyes widening in disgust and horror as she cries, "You killed my son!"

The baker recoils, his eyes sweeping the street to see if her voice has carried.

Her features change again, now softening as she does what until now the baker had only dreamt of her doing: She takes her hands in his and stares lovingly into his eyes. "Adeline," she says. "My baby."

Again the baker flinches. He looks past the judge's wife to the woman's servant, who has kept her eyes on the pavement during this entire scene. "What is the matter with your mistress?"

"Mesmerized, sir. It's addled her brain. She can't seem to recognize a soul rightly, calling them 'Mother' and 'Father' and 'Sister' and 'Son' and 'Lover' when they ain't really no relation at all," the scared-looking girl says, keeping her eyes downcast as the judge's wife, her face a mask of horror and shame, now slaps the baker's face, then backs away, her hands shielding her from his view.

"How can that be?" the baker says to the girl. "I myself have been mesmerized by a trained naturalist, and I do not go about calling my neighbors by strange names."

The judge's wife runs crying out into the muddy street, and the servant girl takes her leave from the baker without another word, to pursue her. This leaves the baker standing in front of the bakery, stunned, dumbfounded, lost. After a few moments he reenters the shop he no longer owns, facing a future he cannot imagine, alone again with memories of castles he has owned, hovels he has died in.

What the baker can't know, not reading the top scientific journals of the day, is that physical theologians have improved the process of mesmerization to the point where an individual can remember not only his or her previous lives, but can also identify those with whom a connection was shared in those lives. Before long, every man sees in every other man—and every other woman and child as well—his mother, father, wife, husband, son, daughter, lover, friend, enemy, killer, savior, rapist, captain, proconsul, slave. Every person has been these and much more to every other, in one or more of the innumerable lives going back to the Garden of Eden.

At first, this creates confusion, even madness, as in the sad case of the judge's wife. But after the newness of this theo-technological breakthrough has worn off, man accepts this new view of man; everyone and everything is connected. There is no one a person has not loved, no one she has not ruled, no one he has not bowed down to. Wars cease over anything but the most urgent crisis, even most quarrels are snuffed out, because no one can murder his beloved mother, sister, and best friend, even for a king's cause. The kings themselves look at their closest advisors and see former enemies, look at their worst enemies and see their own mothers, holding them to their breasts.

It is a memory of a species, a shared memory joining as the limbs of a tree to its trunk as the millennia are retraced.

Within a few years, mathematicians and theoretical theologians take metempsychosis technology to its *ne plus ultra*: the ability of every person to see his lineage of incarnations back to the beginning of human existence, back to the time when there was only one man, the ancestor of all, Adam. With this technique of mesmerization made free and available to the masses, to heads of state and illiterate peasants alike, no one can look at another and not see himself, not see the incarnation they all have in common. All have been the same person, not one's mother or a father or a lover but *the same person*. They remember Adam's life because they lived it: the inspiring touch of God's finger, the incompleteness before Eve, the Garden, the Serpent. It is common knowledge that all souls were once the one Soul, and no one will harm another, because that would be harming oneself. Peace rules the Earth.

In time, however, the kings again desire territory without regard for those who will perish in the fighting; husbands desire mistresses without regard for their wives' suffering; all see and desire and want to attain without reference to some long-ago shared soul. So the technology is banned, naturalists and mesmerists exiled or stoned or burned, the idea of reincarnation officially struck from public record. And so is Man reborn, his soul transmigrating once again, all memory of his former life in Paradise wiped away, all experience of this life encountered without context, a lonely island never in sight of the rest of the living world.

Antemeridian

There is no dinner for the dead. There is no dinner of the bread. There is no winner of the bread. There is no winner in the bed. There is no sinner in the bed. There is no sinner in the red. There is no winter in the red. There is no winter on the road. There is no whimper on the road. There is no whimper from the moat. There is no skipper on the boat. There is no stripper for the load. There is no sipper of the mead. There is no supper for the steed. There is no succour for the need. There is no sucker on the teat. There is no sugar for the tea. There is no ducat for the troupe. There is no glimmer in the head. There is no dinner for the dead.

Maer Hall, Staffordshire, 1838

Three people reposed under the tree at the Wedgwood estate, two of them very much in favor of marriage, one violently opposed. When the two in concord spoke, there were sweet words of interesting conversation, and it made Darwin's heart glad. Anything Emma had said to him kept his mind clear, his gut calm, and his breathing as regular as it could be in proximity to such a beautiful creature.

But the third voice sent Darwin's heart pumping at a nauseating pace, made his head feel near to bursting with worms, and sent the most vile churning through his abdomen. What was worse was that this was a voice only Darwin could hear, and sometimes it drowned out the angelic tones of his beloved.

It belonged to Thomas Malthus. For amusement Darwin had read the Reverend's old book, his *Essay on the Principle of Population*, as he waited for the carriage to come to take him the twenty miles to the Wedgwood Estate. In that short time, Malthus had provided Darwin with the mechanism to explain the transmutation of species that he had been desperately seeking, and sealed his utter commitment to the reality of the dangerous idea.

"Now you see *how* it happens," Malthus said, his voice identical to that of Darwin's father, "how members of populations have to *compete* for resources or be left entirely out of the running—"

"Cousin, you are silent. Is there something you wanted to say to me?" a much more lovely voice interrupted. "To ask me, perhaps?"

It was time. It was time to propose and steer his life on a tack towards respectability and success... and he had not devoted one second to thinking of what he was actually going to say to Emma, how he could show himself to be fit for such a unique resource of happiness.

ԥ ԥ ԥ

"For God's sake, Bobby, don't breathe a word about your atheistic ideas to Cousin Emma," Erasmus Darwin had told his brother that very morning, fussing with Charles's collar against the strict instructions of their dresser.

"I'm a world traveler now, Eras, a known naturalist. Don't call me *Bobby* like I'm ten years old. And my ideas are not atheistic—they follow a Deist—"

"That's all very well, Bob, old man. But whatever you prefer to be called, one thing you will *not* be called is the husband of Cousin Emma, should she hear any of this transubstantiation business."

"*Transmutation*. You know the difference."

"Indeed I do. But your face takes on such a healthy pink sheen when I forget."

Darwin couldn't help but smile at his incorrigible brother, whose brain was used mostly in permanent search of the next bottle to tip and the next bawd to perch upon his lap, but otherwise could be counted on for its uncanny sharpness. "Besides which, I don't plan on discussing my scientific speculations with her," he said.

"I know you don't *plan* on it," Erasmus said, abandoning his work on Charles's necktie. "But I know she interests you because of her lively mind—something not two out of ten ladies possess, I grant you—and you could find yourself saying... *unfortunate* things to her."

"Unfortunate things."

"Don't forget, dear brother, that the Wedgwoods are Christians with a capital *C* and with a capital *H* tossed in for good measure. The women, especially, are Theists, to a man. Or to a woman." He sighed in exasperation with himself. "They're all Theists, Bobby, is what I'm saying, and one word offending that could mean your haunting these halls as a bachelor for another year. Frankly, I can't allow that."

They laughed, and Erasmus continued, "It is good to see you looking so well. I think married life will agree with you."

"It has its advantages, no doubt." In truth, Darwin felt very fine for the first time in a long while.

"Always the practical one, you are. Oh, I think your carriage has arrived"—Erasmus turned and picked up a book off the chest of drawers. "Here's that book you wanted for the ride over. And Bobby?"

Darwin let out a histrionic breath. "Yes?"

"Get Molly to fix your collar. No one would consent to marry such a slubberdegullion."

"Such a *what?*"

"Oh, Bob, you and your pallid knowledge, your pale ontology"—Erasmus cackled at his own wit—"you honestly must crack open a *real* book now and again."

CB　CB　CB

Emma sat transfixed by her cousin's words—they were not at all what she had expected when he asked her for a private meeting under the tree.

"... and that is why, Emma, dear Emma, that I think the divine touch is not needed for every act in the creation of species," he finished, breathing hard now. "I have only just deduced the mechanism—competition and selection of the most fit—but I haven't the slightest idea how it all works."

"Perhaps the Lord does the selection?"

"Perhaps," Darwin said, although to him that was frankly the least interesting option, "but it would be a selection based on law, not on individual supernatural acts."

"But God's Law, surely. Charles, darling"—the last word froze both of them for a moment—"Charles, certainly this is God's Law at work. To proclaim anything else would be speaking with the devil's tongue. Your work... it is an expression of God's Law..." She paused, her eyes meeting his. "Is it?"

"I am certain of it... darling."

Emma modestly examined the laces of her shoes, but with an unmistakable smile.

"This—this *work* is to celebrate the works of God, not to deny them. How much more wonderful is a world in which His will is done by Law than one in which He must constantly intercede and correct Himself! In this way, we see that there are no mistakes—only Law followed to its inevitable ends." He was speaking like the clergyman he was supposed to have become, not as what he had in fact come to be.

Emma, beautiful Emma, considered his words, and after a minute, nodded and looked directly into her cousin's eyes. "You flatter me by sharing your scientific thoughts, Charles. I don't see anything in them that produces the slightest worry in me." She folded her hands on her lap. "Now. Before we

116

rejoin my mother and sisters, was there anything else you wanted to bring up?"

Malthus remained silent. Darwin took this as agreement between himself and the deceased economist, and carried on.

Malthus

In this world, commerce rules all. There is no charity, no altruism. Everything must be earned, everything must be paid in advance.

Baby birds waiting with their mouths open for a meal from their mothers will wait in vain. Only those nestlings that place their beaks so their mother will have a belly itch scratched are rewarded with the food she has flown out and gathered. Those hatchlings unfortunate enough not to happen upon this exchange starve and die. Their little bodies are kept within the nest; no scavengers outside may have a free meal.

Scientists do not share their discoveries with one another for free. Journals must pay top dollar, as *Bentley's Miscellany* or *The Evening Chronicle* do for each installment of the latest Dickens or Trollope. If readers like the theories or announcements made within the pages of scientific journals, then word of mouth brings a rise in sales, full theaters at the writers' lectures, and these names become well known. This is how science succeeds in a world where nothing is given away.

The law of supply and demand keeps ticket prices low for church sermons, and the more fiery the rhetoric, the larger the crowds. Hellfire and brimstone, eternal damnation for the smallest of sins—these are the ingredients of successful theologizing. Occasionally, a vicar—usually a newly minted member of the clergy, filled with idealism and the urge to challenge convention—will offer a free sermon, allow in anyone who cares to come, and then speak to his listeners with kindness, but this is always a failure by definition. For what is to follow a free sermon but another, and another, an endless stream of unprofitable blather? Even if success could be measured in terms other than economic, to what purpose could this success be put? Bread cannot be bought with popularity.

Parks and streams are cordoned off, turnstiles installed. Knowing that others want to visit these places makes those who can afford to get in all the most appreciative of the natural beauty they enjoy. There is no pleasure to be had in what anyone can have. Exclusivity, rarity—these are the highest qualities anything can possess.

To be sure, in this world there are ways to earn that do not directly involve money. Athletes win tournaments and are rewarded with sexual favors from their gaggles of female admirers; inventors create new technologies and are feted with food and wine in addition to their remuneration; naturalists donate their collections to Cambridge and Oxford with the understanding that a hall or a wing will be named in their honor.

But it is all commerce. It is all a race to have or be the highest and the best and the most, whether in money, possessions, fame, infamy, friends, lovers, food and drink, loveliness, fearsomeness, health, knowledge, revenge, salvation, wives or husbands, children, strength, beneficence, power, reputation, victims, longevity, pleasure, pain, foresight, legacy, speed. Those who win survive; those who don't are lost, unremembered, unmourned. It is a race, and no one who falls behind is spared.

Behind the Tortoise are almost all the other racers, unfortunate souls who never made it under their tree to win a wife. Ahead of him there is only the sleeping Hare, proudly draped in epaulets, never giving a second thought in this race to his old friend.

Antemeridian

You aren't supposed to be here in this room of old men nodding in excitement and shaking your hand. They have taken no notice at all of your sloped brow, of the thumbs on your feet, of the nakedness beneath your matted hair; your inappropriateness to indoor society is not a problem, so fascinated are they to meet you. They circle around and stick their noses in your face, caring not that you could bite them right off, something you might just do if they don't back up, give you some air, please, Gentlemen!

You let out a howl that does make them all take a step back from you, widen their circle by a couple of feet, but they are laughing and smiling and pointing, not at all the effect you meant to have. You beat your chest and snarl at them, but they know you now, you are one of them, you are not to be feared, you are theirs now, you are to be held up and admired and beatified and, ultimately, pitied.

Down House, 1843

So this was what industrialization has brought us, FitzRoy mused as he took in the rustic luxury of the foyer of the Darwins' new home in the country. A high birth is no longer a guarantee of wealth or superiority; marrying into a family of factory-owners is enough to lift the son of a doctor over a descendant of kings.

Darwin was a fellow of the Royal Society now; married, with children; and author of a best-selling volume on the voyage of the *Beagle*, while FitzRoy's own three-volume history of the expedition had not sold out its first printing. No wonder the man was constantly sick, he sniffed. Darwin had been rewarded far beyond what his efforts had truly earned. And now, to add to the usurpation by this man who was headed for a country parson's life before FitzRoy plucked him from obscurity, was what Darwin had hinted at in his letters... an origin of species reckoned without God.

It might be another instance of FitzRoy carrying his old friend, but Darwin would be made to see he was on the path to darkness, and be convinced to change tack before he was brought by the lee by the Lord Himself.

"Captain FitzRoy—*Governor* FitzRoy!" Emma called, kissing him on each cheek and rejoicing in his handsome smile. "Dear Robert, amidst all of your busy-ness and success—how good of you to come!"

"The pleasure is mine, Mrs. Darwin." He entered the sitting room and took a seat at Emma's gesture. "The house is looking very well kept, I must say—and it isn't easy to impress a man used to decks scrubbed with holystones."

"You are too good. Of course, I cannot take any credit except as a moral influence on our army of dedicated servants." As she said this, one of the women brought their tea and poured each of them a cup, with a shy smile. "We are blessed to have them."

"Indeed, not even naval officers with medals from the Royal Geographic Society can afford such a staff," he said, watching the girl leave the room. "Where is my old hand, Syms Covington? He has been an invaluable help to your husband, I understand."

"Did Charles not tell you? We have a new man, Parslow. Our beloved Syms has sailed off to settle in Australia!"

"Did he? Ha! I'm afraid that after serving with his mates on the *Beagle*, he will feel all too comfortable surrounded by criminals and savages." They shared a laugh, and FitzRoy shook his head at it all, still smiling. "So. Where is our dear philosopher? I truly wish to see him before I set sail for the antipodes myself."

"Oh, Robert, my letter did not reach you in time! My husband has taken to his bed this last fortnight, sick with... his illness. It gets worse and worse, and he will not tell me the cause, if even he knows it."

FitzRoy let out a breath through his nostrils. "I know the cause."

"So Charles *does* know!" Emma started, her cup shaking on its saucer. "And he has shared this with you?"

"No. No, he hasn't mentioned the sickness at all in our voluminous correspondence, which is what tells me his condition is becoming more grave."

"I see," Emma said, and when FitzRoy did not continue, she added, "But pray, what do you 'know' as the cause of my husband's suffering?"

FitzRoy looked down at his cup, let out another breath, and sipped some tea. "He is a man living two lives."

"What? Surely not—in his condition, he lives barely *one*!"

"His work on the transmutation of species, Emma. Has he not spoken of it to you?"

"Of course he has. He speaks of it incessantly. It is his reigning obsession."

"And you are a woman of God."

"Yes... but what has that—"

"Emma, dear, the idea of transmutation is absolutely *antithetical* to Christianity." FitzRoy put down his cup and saucer and took her hands. "Charles is trying to prove that *there is no God*, that He has no hand in what lives on His Earth."

Emma let out a sweet laugh. "No, you misunderstand! Charles has told me that this research is to prove God's glory. You know the Darwins are Deists, Robert—this transmutation business is a bit of natural theology from the Deist side, that's all. It is anathema to the ears of C of E Theist aristocrats such as yourself, I know"—she chuckled again, warmly, never anything but warmly—"but it is hardly atheism. As he always says, he is simply trying to show the *mechanism* of *how* the Lord brings these creatures about, not *whether* He does or not."

She surprised him with her ready answer to his suspicions, but he could tell that the good child did not see the betraying connection between her husband's "work" and his illness. Solemnly, he leaned in close and said, "That is his secret, Emma. He is taking God out of the picture altogether—he has fooled you, just as he fooled me into taking him around the world so he could gather his blasphemous evidence."

She slipped her hands from his and fixed him with a cold look. "Captain FitzRoy, am I to understand that you stop here on your way to your governorship in order to accuse our Charles of atheism and blasphemy?"

FitzRoy froze. Although he never would have put it into exactly those words, she could not have hit the mark more perfectly.

"I remind you, sir, that if it weren't for his illness— contracted on *your* voyage—he would have entered the life of the clergy upon his return. He is no atheist! He..." She could not continue, and worked to stifle a sob.

"Emma, dear Emma, it's only that I am worried about your husband—my friend—and how, as he lives the comfortable life of the wealthy industrialist, and the satisfying life of a best-selling naturalist, he might be losing sight of the most important goal: *Salvation*."

She looked at him again. "You think his research is leading him away from Salvation?"

"That is my speculation and my fear: that Charles is getting more and more ill because he must lie to himself, and perhaps unconsciously to you and to me, about this *transmutation* business. He knows in his heart of hearts that it is godless, and that will make him a man dying on the inside as long as he hides this from himself and from others. As Matthew says: A house divided against itself cannot stand."

He had hoped to say these words to Darwin himself, let him know that although his material wealth was great and his scientific stature was growing—while his former confidante and captain, a descendant of Charles II, applied and scrounged

for work before being named governor of a far-off colony—
that his material success would not be enough at the time of
Judgment.

Emma seemed to take this in for a few minutes, staring
through tear-reddened eyes at a spot on the wall behind Fitz-
Roy, finally saying, "Charles promised me he had mentioned
these ideas to no one but you and myself. I *made* him promise,
because he has written a small treatise and told me to have it
published in the event of his death."

"You read it, then? You know what these ideas are?"

She stiffened. "I do not open sealed envelopes not addressed
to me, sir. But I told him I would not follow his wishes if he
did not take me into his confidence."

"But no one else knows of these heretical speculations?"

Emma started with a sigh, "Robert, I cannot say for certain—" but now her eyes widened as she spotted something
near the floor behind FitzRoy, and her face broke into a smile.
"Ah! It seems that our Charles will be joining us after all!"

FitzRoy turned and saw a chubby little girl—no more than
two years old, toddling around the side of his chair and looking behind herself with gleeful anticipation—then turned back
to Emma with a quizzical half-smile and said jocularly, "He
seems shorter."

Emma laughed. "Wherever his precious Annie is, her father will not be far behind," she said, and her prediction was
on the mark: not ten seconds after the little one trundled to
her mother, the pale visage and weakened body of her father,
dressed in a nightgown and robe, appeared in the doorway. In
his slow and feeble way, he had been playing at chase with his
daughter!

FitzRoy laughed and stood. "Charles, she *must* be your favorite if she got you out of a sickbed, one that even your old
Captain could not rouse you from."

"Ho! Little Annie pulled on my bedcovers and teased me into following her down the stairs—she's the one who knew there was an important guest!" Darwin said with a wheezy laugh and embraced FitzRoy, then eased himself onto the settee between his wife's chair and his friend's. Annie immediately clambered up to sit on his lap. "But for goodness' sake, don't tell her she's my favorite—she's an advantage-seeking rapscallion enough as it is!"

The three adults laughed, and little Annie pulled on Darwin's mutton chop.

"So, you've had your stint in Parliament, served as Conservator of the Mersey, and now you're off as Governor of New Zealand. When you return, you'll be named prime minister, no doubt," Darwin said, as Annie stood perched on his leg. "And I will still be here, a useless, knobby tree for wayward children to climb."

"I have moved about positions, it's true," FitzRoy said, meeting Emma's eyes for an instant, then added, "But what are you doing with yourself these days, Charles? Your *Zoology of the Beagle* is to the publisher at last, and you've gotten your carcasses and bones from whence you sent them—"

"Oh yes, a room full. They'll be years in the sorting out."

"Aye, of course." FitzRoy let the silence bloom. Finally he said, "Charles, I come here not only out of a wish to see you, but also to share a concern."

"Concern?"

He cleared his throat. "You have written to me a great deal about this 'transmutation' idea."

"Ha!" Darwin laughed, but his eyes did not seem to share in the mirth. "Yes, I must admit the idea still intrigues me. Do you remember our conversations on the ship, our back-and-forth over why this animal was created, from where did fossils originate, those endless discussions of how Nature works, and how she might be persuaded to share her secrets?"

"Certainly I do."

"That's all it is, Robert. Speculations, a mental hobby. Nothing to worry about."

"But are *you* worried, my friend?" FitzRoy asked. "About where this research is taking you?"

Darwin's smile faltered, and he set Annie gently down on the floor. "I have said nothing of 'research,' my friend—only of ideas. Surely ideas are not blasphemous."

"Please don't take offense if I note that *you* are the first to use that word."

Darwin had looked pale upon entering the room; now he was positively green. "Please excuse me—I believe another attack is on its way. Robert, safe voyage." He perfunctorily shook hands with FitzRoy, then stumbled out of the room and clomped up the stairs, shutting the door behind him before Annie could follow.

FitzRoy stood and said, "He is a man with a secret, Emma. And the secret is that he is losing faith in God."

In response, Emma merely rested her gaze on little Annie, trying to clamber onto the first stair to go after her father. "Charles could never lose faith in the God who gave him Annie," she said, "no matter how beaks and barnacles may try to lead him astray."

Lamarck

In this world, time is measured by increasing complexity.

Single-celled protists, the simplest creatures possible, generate from nothingness, and immediately begin their long trek up the cliffs of improvement. With each strike of solar rays, each shake of the Earth, each encounter with another organism, the protist folds and divides, develops, always moving forward, its complexity jumping.

They turn to bacteria, then to plankton, then to ambulatory organisms, to crustaceans, to squid, to fish, to frogs, to lizards, to mice, to cats, to horses, to humans. Or, if the sun's rays hit them a different way, they turn from fungus to kelp, to grass, to ferns, to flower bushes, to trees. Or water turns to foam, to mud, to sand, to rock, to hill, to mountain, to mountain with fossils, to mountain with seashells.

Everything in this world evolves by increasing in complexity; there is no information ever lost, only made inaccessible, as it changes from idea to gesture, to symbol, to language, to number, to abstract number, to code, to unbreakable code, to code without key.

People, too, in this world hurry to accomplish their tasks before the jobs become unmanageably complex, too difficult

133

to be performed by someone as little evolved as they. A woman cracks eggs, preparing to break them into a bowl; but the arrival of the morning post interrupts her. By the time she returns to the kitchen, the eggs have re-formed with a tough new honeycombed outer shell which must be broken in a particular way, with a particular egg-breaking tool she does not own—but which her neighbor does.

Unworried, she pops next door and borrows the tool from her friend, smiling at herself as she reenters her kitchen. The smile falls from her face, however, as she positions the tool inside one of the honeycomb cells and realizes that the tool requires steam power, something she hadn't noticed when she first took possession of it five minutes earlier. What a ridiculous contraption—to use it, one would need a steam engine in one's own home!

She decides to make her husband something else for breakfast, since this has become too complicated. But when she moves to toss the unbroken eggs onto the compost, she sees that the honeycomb shell has seeped like candle wax onto a letter she had been rereading, a letter from her lover, the man who will be arriving that day to take her away, arriving just hours after her naval lieutenant husband is to embark on a year-long Mediterranean voyage.

She hears him on the stairs, coming down to breakfast, and frantically tries to remove the letter from the counter, but the melted egg shell has hardened like a clear lacquer, sealing the letter like a mosquito in amber, the amorous words and plans frozen and readable. How will she hide the letter? Or explain it? Terrible!

Her husband is on the last step now. Panicked, the woman breaks a whale-oil lamp against the zinc counter and strikes a wooden match, instantly filling the kitchen with flame and smoke. She makes a dash for the back door, turning just in time to see the flames lick up the wooden wall behind the cabinet and also see her husband hurl his coat against the fire, smothering it.

The kitchen counter is melted and black, all signs of the letter gone. The woman breathes a sigh of relief and allows her soon-to-be-hoodwinked husband to take her into his arms. "Never worry, my dear. I shall put off my departure for twenty-four hours, catch the tide tomorrow," he says. "I must write to our agent and see—"

"No!" she cries. Her lover is to arrive that very day! How will she explain the stranger's presence to her husband? How will she explain her *husband's* continued presence to her lover? Awful!

Her next-door neighbor, the husband of the friend with the egg-breaking machine, rushes through the gate, followed by several other neighborhood men, all concerned at the commotion. After seeing she is all right, they lead her husband back into the house to inspect the damage, leaving her to meander into the front garden to recover.

Just then a carriage arrives in front of the house, and a dashing young man steps out. He calls to the woman, who freezes at the sound of his "Darling!" She turns and sees her lover striding up to her. He takes her into his arms and envelops her into a deep kiss before she can warn him to stop. Their lips part, and that is when the woman notices the crowd that has come out of the front door, staring at them, her husband in the front, his mouth agape.

She shuts her eyes, trying in vain to think of something to say, *anything*. When she opens them, the first thing she sees, something she has never before noticed, is that on her lover's finger, looking like it has been worn for years, is a wedding band, a ring of new complications.

Antemeridian

I am the essence of man, traveling by his seed, into the awaiting egg. The egg is what gives the embryo form; the sperm is what gives it a name, individuality, a soul. To be man is to know; to be woman is simply to be.

If I am flooded into you and hear your heart beat from inside, how can I be other than you? If I meet your form and begin there, how is it that I can change? What are we, if not one?

The salty womb swirls around me, inside you. I can see your face in the warm dark. How can I hurt you if we are one? How can we be one if I hurt you? I hear your voice in the deep, and it calms me.

Am I the fish, the snake, the ape, the sperm, the egg? Am I the son of the bird, the frog, of beetle, of human, of woman, of salt water, of blood? Are you the mother of the bird, the barnacle, the dinosaur, the sea, the moon, the sun?

I am an electric dynamo with the factory, spinning in place and drawing energy from the immediate environment in order to generate it perpetually for the world outside. I am a greased cog winding in the machine, in the gears of your womb. Your machine has churned since the beginning of time, producing widgets of life, producing automata with name and form and eyes to see.

Down House, 1846

There was but one specimen left from the voyage of the *Beagle* to be analyzed, and it had promised to be quick work: a barnacle, the smallest ever found. It lived parasitically inside of a conch shell Darwin had found ten years earlier on the beach in southern Chile, and all he had to do was describe and classify it. Once this little job was done, he thought, the adventure of his life would truly be finished, and he could turn his thoughts to what to do about his transmutation ideas. He still had only the treatise in the envelope he had given to Emma years before to show for all his tortured thought; still, since he had handed that over and focused on finishing the categorizing of the last animals and insects, he had taken the water cure, diminishing his illness, and he was able to play with the children for relatively long stretches of time. Annie was turning out the most darling child of all, sometimes accompanying him on his rambles on the path behind the house, her little hands clasped behind her in solemn imitation of her father, which made Darwin's eyes sting from the effort not to laugh.

But barnacles. Barnacles. The little ill-formed monsters had not proved as tractable as he had foolishly assumed they would be. The scientific world knew very little about these creatures, in fact long mistaking them for mollusks, when in fact they were crustaceans, closer to crabs than to snails. The particular aberration left over from the *Beagle* he named *Anthrobalanus*, and hated the name as much as he came to hate the specimen itself.

His hatred of the tiny bastard came from its hold over Darwin's life. Over the previous six months, he had been forced to contact conchologists, museums, even active sea-captains in his search for more barnacles, in order to find commonalities and differences between the thousands of vari-eties in the world. His study was filling with barnacles, barna-cles, barnacles; they clung to him as if he were an old three-masted barque that had been moored, then forgotten.

As he worked on describing and classifying them over the months, however, Darwin realized that the little buggers rep-resented an unmatched opportunity: If he could become known for truly and exhaustively presenting an important species to the scientific world, then he would himself be newly classified—as an authority in biology. And with that kind of renown, he would come from a higher position when the time came to re-lease his theory of the origin of species. In fact, he could work on his barnacles in the morning, and after his lunch, a walk, and a nap, work on his transmutation ideas in the afternoon, each task supporting the other.

With this thought in mind, he tucked in to the morning's specimens, and worked steadily until Parslow announced lunch, and brought the day's post.

Darwin took his letters from the offered tray. As usual, they were mostly invitations to meetings, dinners, ceremo-nies—to all of which he would send his regrets, begging off by citing his illness, which had at least served that one purpose over the years. Then there were a few scientific scribblings from his fellows at the Royal Society, even a tiny box no doubt containing a curious new barnacle found by one of his correspondents. And at the bottom was a letter posted from Wellington, on government stationery. *Robert!* With relish, Darwin slit this letter open, leaving the invitations for Emma and the rest for later.

His eyes scanned the single page. When he finished reading, his heart heavy, he sank back into his chair and let out a heavy breath.

FitzRoy had been dismissed as Governor of New Zealand. His attempts to reconcile the claims of the white settlers with the land rights of the native Maori had proved an embarrassment and a disaster; Darwin had heard as much, from Fitz-Roy's own letters as well as from newspaper accounts. The governor had become reviled by one side for his liberality— *Oh, the irony!* Darwin thought about his Tory captain—and disrespected by the other for his perceived weakness, as the Maori valued toughness over anything else, even fairness. They would rather be killed than coddled, FitzRoy had written, and they thought that a white man standing up for their rights was coddling of the most condescending sort.

Another opportunity, another failure. Darwin thought of his noble friend and felt towards him, for the very first time, a twinge of pity.

Linnaeus

In this world, taxonomy is more than mere classification. It is reality. The lines between each and every member of a species, or genus, or phylum, or family, or kingdom are traceable, literally visible, connecting all living things with one another as well as with their ancestors.

And the lines are rigid. Species are not collections of animals lumped together because of some perceived regularity; they are actual, hard divisions between creatures. There is no platypus here, straddling lines and confusing naturalists—or rather, there *is* a platypus, but even a casual examination of the threads connecting it to other creatures (as well as to its progenitors) reveals that it is of the family *Ornithorhynchidae*, genus *Ornithorhynchus*, in fact its only member. That is what it actually *is*, its essence. In this world, there is little more real science has to say about any creature, once its place is found in the taxonomic scheme; describing its behavior or dietary preferences or how it cares for its young is work for psychology, sociology—the soft sciences, not biology.

Here is the spider, and its phylum mate, the hermit-crab. Pray, how do we know they are of the same taxonomic category? Pay no mind to their common jointed feet or their ex-

143

ternal skeletons; these are literal surface similarities, something any corner sketch artist untrained in science could put together. No, we must shine our light on their Tendrils of Linnaeus, shining like silk as they stretch from the essence of one animal to the other. What is this essence? Why does it shine when exposed to certain hues of incandescence? How are these connections at once unbreakable, but at the same time utterly permeable? Leave those questions to the philosophers; we are scientists. It is our job to classify, to follow and map the Tendrils linking every creature to every other.

It is not only in the world of biology that these links can be roused into giving light—here is the sea-captain and his crew, aboard their brig in the middle of the Atlantic. Again, how do we know their true classification, as prescribed by Nature? And again, pay no attention to the marks of rank stitched onto their uniforms; these are mere epiphenomena, more important to dressmakers than to scientists. Look to the Linnaean threads linking the Captain to the lower examples of his genus, the lieutenants, the able seamen, the loblolly boys. Now look especially carefully, off the stern... reflecting the luminous foam in the ship's wake are thin filaments connecting each man on board with the men above them, the Admiralty back in England. Their threads connect them like marionettes up to the House of Lords, and theirs up to the Royal Family. We have not been granted permission to examine the Queen's Tendrils of Linnaeus, once rumored to be connected only—

But no. That is theology, not science.

The work of biology is almost finished. Once every extant animal has been classified according to its true connection to all other forms of life, past and present, there will be no more for biologists to do. We will know where every animal, every insect, and fish, and bacterium, belongs in the hierarchy of existence.

In the world of humans, too, we will know for a fact what men are higher and what men are lower, who is born to be a winner, and who has usurped another's proper place in the scheme of things. Who is connected, and who is not.

Antemeridian

God is not here and I am alone.

I know this is Heaven but I do not know my way around.

They speak only Classical Greek and Latin here.

I am a wound, a blister, a blight who has not studied.

Annie is not here and God is not here and I am alone with these scholars.

They wear the *toga vīrilus*.

I wear the *toga prætextra*, its purple sash like a screamed excuse.

Emma is not here and Annie is not here and God is not here and I am alone by the sacred fountain from which I dare not drink.

They drink wine diluted with water here, served in shallow bowls.

I want to drink from the sacred fountain, but they watch me.

They know I look for God here and smirk at me, nodding to one another.

Annie was just here and Emma was just here, but you have missed them, I am told in Greek that I do not understand,.

Do not drink from the sacred fountain, I am told in Latin.

God was here until He was murdered in His bed by a trusted servant, I am told in East-Aramaic.

Where have they gone? I ask in English.

We do not understand you, the scholars answer, also in English. *Do not bathe in the sacred fountain.*

Annie is here, wearing the *stola* of a married woman.

Emma is here, but I cannot see her.

Annie speaks Latin to me, then Greek, then English, pointing to a bearded man. I cannot understand her and do not know she is trying to introduce her husband.

I do not understand that this is your husband, I say in the chittering squeaks of a female dolphin. *You are ten years old and a widow.*

God is here, but I cannot see Him.

Down House, 1849

Three years of barnacles, and Darwin had made it through no more than a third of the specimens. Falling asleep at night, before the strange dreams appeared, he saw larval barnacles dancing before his eyes, felt adults latched onto his lids, and smothered under the weight of them all over his skin. They fascinated him, and they kept his mind off of FitzRoy's ongoing plight, now as superintendent of the Royal Naval Dockyards, now running sea trials for someone else's ship, the HMS *Arrogant*.

FitzRoy on the *Arrogant*. Darwin smirked at the idea, and was heartily ashamed of himself.

"What's funny, Papa?"

Darwin started in his chair—Annie had been so quietly playing by his desk that he had forgotten she was in the room. "My! Nothing is funny, my dear."

"That's not true. Lots of things are funny!"

Now a real smile warmed Darwin's face. He loved Annie's way of turning phrases around and showing the absurdity of the things adults said to children. On the few occasions that he and Emma had guests at Down House, Annie was sure to amuse them with her wordplay and general sweetness. She was one of those girls who was the brightest spot in any room. At the age of eight, she had never in her young life performed an action that required punishment of any kind. She and goodness were one.

He turned in his chair to face his daughter. "Tell me something that's funny."

The tip of Annie's tongue poked out between her teeth as she reached into her sharp little mind for a trinket that might enchant her father. "Barnacles are crustaceans, is that not true?" she said, mimicking the legalistic query Darwin sometimes used in teaching logical reasoning to the children.

"I cannot deny it."

"And barnacles fasten themselves to the outsides of ships, is that also true?"

"To their *hulls*, yes indeed. Forming a thick skin, layers upon layers sometimes."

"And the ships convey these over the world?"

"Also true."

Annie's lips curled up at the sides, a sure sign that she was about to apply her fatal blow. "So one could say that these *crustaceans* are *crust agents* that have *crossed oceans*."

Darwin banged his fist against the desk and bent double with laughter. "Very good! *Jolly* good, Annie darling!" When he looked at her again, Annie's eyes were wet with pride and mirth.

"Mama says that I have your wit, and your nose."

"Does she?" Darwin said, still laughing. "As usual, she is on the mark. At least about the sense of humor—but I was never as clever a child as you are. Perhaps you have picked it up from playing by my side while I work all these years."

"But what about your nose?"

"I make you a promise: You may have my nose whenever I am not using it."

Annie clapped in delight, stood to give her father a kiss, and returned to the floor to scribble in one of Darwin's water-damaged blank notebooks. Darwin gazed at her for a few moments, thankful for the blessing she was, and got back to work himself.

Saint-Hilaire

In this world, acquired characteristics are inherited.

Here one sees the newly married or those in search of beaus constantly striving at self-improvement, not only to give important qualities to their children but also to be judged good potential mothers and fathers, people who will stretch and study and avoid danger in order to make taller, smarter, more complete descendants.

Posture is vitally important; slouching will be passed on, giving children a beastly appearance, so all walk as peacocks, heads high, preening for their opposite number. Medical examinations by a qualified naturalist are *de rigueur* for potential couples even before a first date, for who wants to waste time on someone with a hidden, but all too inheritable, defect? A missing toe, a bum knee, hemorrhoids?

But for those who pass the test, marriage and mating take place almost immediately. The world is too dangerous to allow lovers to wait—a fall from a horse could alter one's nose permanently; a bite from a spider could cause discoloration; the chop from a misaimed axe could result in myriad disasters. So they couple as soon as possible, taking advantage of their perfection.

The lonely ones, the unlucky ones, are easy to spot. They have some obvious defect, some deviation from the norm, that makes them unmarriageable. A veteran with one sleeve pinned up to his shoulder. A woman whose face was burned in a kitchen fire. Even a man with a vacant stare, as if he's seen something too horrible to forget. All of these are damaged goods, and will never find a lover, at least not until they are too old to make babies, too old to pass on their acquired flaws.

Sometimes, however, the flawed find ways to compensate, and locate mates with whom they can cancel out the physical injuries that have befallen them. A beautiful woman, young and perfect in every respect except that she is missing her left foot, lost in a carriage accident, meets a man missing his right foot. They visit the naturalist stationed in their town, and he blesses their union; their child will be born with both feet, although they will be unusually small. But the child may then compensate by marrying a mate with very large feet (perhaps flattened and splayed by too much walking), and all will even out for *their* children.

People marry and mate very young here, of course, the better to begin the work of producing offspring before any accidents may befall them, altering their appearance or limiting their function. Thus, by their early teens, most of those who will find mates have found them, and by their mid-twenties, they are grandparents, elders of their clans. Marriages may be voluntarily dissolved upon the birth of a grandchild, because no more children will be born to people this old. Even here, acquired characteristics rule the day: For after generation upon generation of those over twenty-five or thirty refraining from conception—for fear of children inheriting scars, broken fingers, deafness in one ear—the *ability* to conceive has now been lost to people over this age.

Far from being a tragedy, however, this results in untold freedom for anyone beyond child-rearing years. Because adolescence and very early adulthood is now the time filled with work to produce and support a family, most thirty-year-olds are retired from careers, freed from marriage, supported materially and socially by generations of descendants who fill the shops and streets with commerce and bustle.

The elders can now turn to education, something not afforded the young in their hurry to mate before they suffer some disfigurement. They take classes, spar in debates, ride horses and explore caves, all with a new indifference to scars and acquired idiosyncrasies, physical or mental. Let the teens worry about their appearance to a mate; in this world, life begins at thirty!

These elders also engage in sex. Having fulfilled the responsibilities of marriage and child-rearing, the elders may now indiscriminately and without worry fornicate with whomever they please, whenever they please. Pregnancy is an impossibility to those so old, and marriage is a now-unnecessary limitation of options, but their bodies are still strong and still full of desire and stamina. Free sexual expression goes hand-in-glove with cavalier risk to life and limb: It is a daring leap into the expanse of possibility without reference to what one might owe anyone else.

But as the bodies grow wrinkled and gray, and the sexual urge fades, what rises to the top is a connection unrelated to sex, procreative or otherwise. By the age of seventy-five, the average person is a great-great-great-grandparent, the matriarch or patriarch of a grand clan, and knows well the depth and breadth of family connection, of affection without any recourse to the physical. Having slept with perhaps dozens, even hundreds of people since the dissolution of one's marriage, an elder is connected to almost everyone in the village through the act of sex; lovemaking is no more of an important connection than are conversation or friendship. Jealousy and self-preservation have been lost in this world. Acquired, in their stead, is love.

Antemeridian

Annie barnacles.

Barnacles in drawers, barnacles in teapots, barnacles in vest pockets, barnacles in my mouth, barnacles in barnacles, very barnacles.

Little mucose barnacles, jointed, sticky. Vertiginous barnacles for sale by natives. Portuguese barnacles are barnacles.

Cetology knows barnacles. Ask a whale for his backside, barnacles in a chamber pot. Topside, barnacles in his hair.

Barnacles salty taste. If a barnacle, for Christ's sake.

Rosary field of barnacles, pebbles beach of barnacles, hand wounds of barnacles, blood of barnacles, white blood flowing for the sin of clinging white grapes crushed for barnacle wine. Vintage is eternity of the sea, a very good year.

My seed is flowing barnacles. Flood the womb, take root, grow segmented joints, form a thousand million species, die stuck to rocks.

Whither barnacles? Wither barnacles. Winter barnacles. Vintner barnacles. Splinter barnacles. Splendor barnacles. Tremble barnacles. Terror barnacles. Error barnacles. Arrow barnacles. Annie barnacles.

Do barnacles dream of legs? Do barnacles dream of me?

Great Malvern, 1851

"This is her inheritance," Darwin muttered to Doctor Gully, as the nurse wiped up the green bile that was all Annie could bring up now. "This is my gift to her."

"Mister Darwin, do keep up hope. You may recall that your own stomach troubles were diminished by our waters here. We have performed miracles before; I daresay we shall do so again."

Miracles, Darwin repeated to himself, and stared into Annie's glassy eyes. It was a miracle she was still alive, after falling to fevers and stomach pain the year before, unable to eat and barely able to move. He had brought her to Gully, who had used the water cure—as well as a strict proscription against work on his barnacles—to miraculously help alleviate Darwin's physical woes. He also couldn't work on his transmutation ideas during that time, since he had none of his notes or materials with him at Malvern.

But Annie had no such work or secrets; she had nothing but goodness and light, and now here she was, laid low by the same ailment from which her father suffered, but much worse. Amplified, as if it were a trait selected by livestock breeders in both parents.

Darwin's eyes stung from the effort not to cry. Annie's mother had no condition like this—no, this curse was passed down entirely from her father. No breeder would have chosen a sire with such a horrific dominant characteristic.

His daughter's watery blue eyes sparked to life for a moment, and found Darwin's. And before slipping once again into her haze of pain, she gave her father a tiny, but unmistakable, smile.

"We have done all we can do, medically," Gully said, not noticing the catch in Darwin's breath. "All we can do now is pray."

The word snapped Darwin's attention onto the doctor. "Pray?"

"Your dear wife waits at home, eight months along, in terrible anxiety. You will have a new child soon whether or not Ann recovers, Charles. Pray for your child here, pray for your child there. What science cannot provide, God will," he said, and stepped from the room, avoiding another glance at the patient or her father.

ඏ   ඏ   ඏ

When the sun rose the next morning, Easter morning, it shined through the window onto a man on his knees, resting his elbows on his daughter's bed, in the same position he had maintained since the nurse had left ten hours earlier.

In the first watch of the night, Charles Darwin begged God not to take Annie, to return her to those who loved and needed her. She had done no wrong, not ever; and even if she were finally going to play with the angels in Heaven, surely her family could be allowed to keep her and love her into adulthood, see her own children born.

The moonlight showed her face an even more deathly pale.

In the second watch, Darwin begged God to take him instead. His work on barnacles was nearly complete; the world of science could finish it without him. The world of science meant nothing to him compared to his love for his dear Annie. And even though, if God took him, he would not see Annie grow into the kind and gentle woman he knew she would become, it would be well worth it to know on his deathbed that she would live. Please, Lord. Please.

She choked and coughed up the tiny bit of gruel she had taken, then again lay still.

In the last watch of the night, with the black sky hinting at purple, Darwin promised God that he would destroy his transmutation research if He let Annie live. His notes, the envelope he had given to Emma, the treatise he had sent in secrecy to his most trusted colleague, everything. He would cease work on the barnacles, cease work on anything remotely related to the origin or development of species, burn it all. He would take up the life of the clergyman he was meant to become all those years ago; he would spread God's Word, His Truth, to anyone and everyone he encountered for the rest of his life, if God would only bring his Annie back from the edge of death, bring her back to health and to life.

In the third watch of the night, he heard FitzRoy's words as clearly as if the Captain were kneeling right beside him: *If you ever are in real need, all you must do is appeal to our Lord, pray to Him with a pure heart. And He will provide.*

Darwin was now in real need. He prayed with the purest heart he had. He opened himself to what God would provide. He put his full faith and trust in the Lord.

Three days later, her body twisted in agony, Annie died.

Lyell

In this world, Lyell is right: Species don't transmute. When individuals are no longer fit enough for their environment, they cease to exist, replaced by other beings until species entirely new arise. This is called "the vanishing."

This is a world in which obsolescence does not exist, because the obsolete do not exist; they disappear, and are replaced. Perhaps there is a master Replacer at work, or perhaps it is a completely natural process, but ultimately it doesn't matter; when an individual no longer belongs in this world, it vanishes entirely, somewhere supplanted by another being at that exact moment. There is no time to say goodbye, because anyone could become unfit, unworthy of existence, at any time whatsoever. The breeze blows in an unusual direction, and a village existing in fresh air is erased; earthquakes shake an entire class of insect into nonexistence; an undiagnosable illness reduces families member by member during the long night.

The problem is that no one knows what this "fitness" could be, what qualities a being possesses or fails to possess that renders it extant or extinct. No one knows what makes a beloved daughter evaporate, her place taken immediately by a new baby. Or why hope vanishes one day, leaving only a brand-new despair in its stead. Or why the saurians died out, mammals suddenly filling the world in their absence. Or what erased the race of stooped *homo habilus*, making space for upright *homo erectus*.

Loss of the vital and its replacement with the lesser is not confined only to living things. People simply stopped using the spinning wheel when the industrial loom appeared, one disappearing while the other took over. But where the spinning wheel allowed a woman quiet time for introspection and quality of craft for her family, the loom is a steam-driven machine, weaving noise and pollution along with its anonymous product. There was no *transmutation* from the wheel to the loom; one fine species died out, and another, more fit, less enchanting one filled the niche. But as for *why* the loom arose and the wheel vanished, there are only vague notions of economics, worker migration patterns, theoretical family dynamics, nothing of any solidity, nothing applying to any one person who has lost her grandmother's cherished spinning wheel and now must break her back, away from home, over a gnashing loom.

Scientists make hypotheses, but they can't be tested except retroactively, giving a "just so" explanation for anything that disappears and is replaced. Mammoths popped out of being, and modern elephants popped in—well, they must have been unfit for a change in the climate. A niche cannot remain unfilled, so elephants popped into being, Mammoth-like animals that, by definition, must have been more fit for the new environment. But these explanations don't actually *explain* anything, and leave science frustrated and embarrassed. Without guidance from the scientific world they had grown to trust, people try to make their own solutions to the vanishing— fighting illness through denial, refusing to accept replacement individuals and species, even killing them as they appear— desperate measures that do nothing but heighten misery.

The Church issues edicts stating that "the vanishing" is due to God's immediate need for certain souls in His war against Satan. But this begs the question: Are these replacement beings less worthy, less valuable to God, than those which had been suddenly called to His side? The inescapable answer— *yes*—leaves the Church frustrated and embarrassed. Without help from the elders with whom they had once practiced their faith, people make their own religion of trying to appease this thieving God—they sacrifice anything they think He will take instead of what is most valuable to them, burning their unneeded possessions, exiling less beloved family members, even slicing their own throats—and the suffering multiplies.

Everyone, everywhere, is swept up by the vanishing. No one can understand it, and so no one can stop it. No doctor can save a child who has somehow become unfit for life, and she leaves her family bereft; no Luddite can stop machines from multiplying where handmade things used to live, and the world becomes colder by the day. No prayer, no vaccine, nothing will keep anything here one instant past its time.

A world without transmutation is a world without rescue from despair.

But if, instead, all beings and things could be shown to transmute, to change, to *evolve* from one state to another instead of simply vanishing and being replaced —if this could be shown, then people could at least understand *why* everything they love will one day be stripped from them, understand *how* the middling supplants the fine. And through this grasping of the *mechanism* of transmutation, whatever it may be, the world could escape its endless despair. It could finally see that this all-knowing, all-powerful, all-benevolent God—He who promises so much and delivers so little—is neither wise, nor strong, nor good, if indeed He exists at all.

Antemeridian

Mount Darwin.

Moruloidea darwinii.

Darwin Sound.

Rhinoderma darwinii.

Darwin University.

Berberis darwinii.

Darwinshire. Darwinford. East Darwinia.

Mylodon darwinii.

"We've decided to name the baby 'Charles.' Yes, after the great man."

Chionelasmus darwinii.

Darwin's Comet. Asteroid Darwin.

Homo darwinii.

Darwin, the ninth planet of the solar system.

Universus darwinii.

M111, the Darwin Galaxy.

Deus darwinii.

Annie Darwin.

The Royal Society, London, 1855

"Another medal for you, Charles," FitzRoy said before the circle of men, his languid tone belied by a quivering of his aristocratic chin. "The study of barnacles has saved many lives, never doubt it."

Darwin's stomach lurched. He hadn't seen FitzRoy but twice since Annie's funeral, and now his old Captain resembled nothing more closely than a tall ship in disrepair—rudderless, with formerly taut cables fallen slack, and masts still bent against an opposing wind that had long died away.

"Eight years with the little creatures, showing how they are related to other little creatures," FitzRoy continued, "and how none of them ever suffered Creation by God."

"Robert—"

"Good gracious, Mister FitzRoy!" the man to Darwin's left, Doctor Lyell, interrupted Darwin, nearly by shouting. "Let us not bring *God* into the picture to create strife! You were elected a fellow of this Society thanks to the favor of this man whose achievements you belittle."

"I am *Captain* FitzRoy, sir, on the seniority list for rear admiral! Head of the Meteorological Department, devising forecasts to save sailors' lives!"

"Gentlemen—"

"Yes, yes. You are the lucky seaman who has made a career out of light reflected by his ship's esteemed naturalist. The pseudo-scientist who now amuses Britain with his daily guesses at the weather of the next day."

FitzRoy's chin no longer quivered; now his entire body shook with rage and indignation as his rheumy eyes fixed on the Doctor's throat. "If this were the time before Her Majesty's reign, I would demand satisfaction from you, sir."

Darwin stepped into the circle, physically blocking the two men's view of each other. He swallowed his gorge and said forcefully, "Gentlemen, I *insist* that you stop this immediately! You are causing embarrassment in this learned Society."

FitzRoy, the old cat, looked as if he might leap past Darwin and pounce on Lyell, but after a few tense seconds, dropped his gaze and said, "My apologies, Charles."

Lyell muttered an apology to Darwin and then to FitzRoy as well, but added, "However, I do stand by my statement that there is no need to bring God into a scientific discussion."

Darwin looked beseechingly into FitzRoy's eyes, and the Captain—amazingly—remained calm, nodding at him with something approaching a reassuring smile. Darwin let out a breath in relief, and shuffled back to his spot in the circle of men, but he did not reclaim his place before another fellow, Charles Hood, said loudly, "Perhaps, since it is his work that seems to bring forth such a question, we should ask our guest of honor *his* opinion on the place of God in science."

All eyes in the circle—indeed, in the room—turned to Darwin, and his mouth dried up completely, unable to form any words to beat back their stares. FitzRoy, who just a moment before was a balm to Darwin's nerves, now looked at him expectantly, waiting for a particular answer that surely he knew better than to give, even under the pressure of his colleagues, for being held to either position would be a disaster.

Finally he emitted a feeble "Excuse me——" and turned from the group. He stumbled two paces before doubling over, vomiting under a table, and plummeting into blissful unconsciousness.

ଔ   ଔ   ଔ

The face of Darwin's old God was gazing at him when he opened his eyes an hour later, splayed on a leather divan in what he recognized as the library of the Society. "Robert," he wheezed, "I have offended thee."

"Do not discomfort yourself, my friend," FitzRoy seated on the edge, said gently, "for I am the one entirely in the wrong here. I beg your forgiveness."

Darwin managed a smile. "We have known one another far too long to beg forgiveness or to grant it. We started off as young pups scrapping over fossils, and now we are old fossils ourselves, growling at each other from across the kennel."

FitzRoy smiled in return and said, "I am a bitter old man, Charles. This world has made a mockery of me."

"Certainly not." With FitzRoy's help, he sat up a bit. "You are a hair's breadth from knighthood, for all the service you have given this nation. I, for one, do not mock the work you have done in meteorological statistics. You have indeed saved many lives, while my barnacles are utterly——"

"Your barnacles have enchanted scientists throughout the world. This world has embraced you and your work. And rightfully so, old man." FitzRoy patted Darwin on the arm and gazed off into the room. "Besides, you are welcome to it. I am focused now on the next world."

"The next world?" Darwin asked as if he had no inkling to his friend's meaning, but immediately thoughts of FitzRoy's uncle, the suicidal Viscount Castlereagh, flashed through his mind. "Is that not quite a bit... premature? You married again only last year. She has given you yet another daughter to cherish."

"Of course, Philos, of course. I don't plan to shuffle off this mortal coil as yet. But, as my dear, departed Mary waits for me in Heaven, I admit—I do spend my days looking forward to my union with God."

Darwin stroked his beard and thought deeply before speaking. "Do not speak like this, Robert. You have much yet to accomplish."

"Ah, but that were true. I captained the most successful surveying mission in history, and but two decades later I am the butt of jokes, lampooned in the very newspapers that once published my weather forecasts." He looked into Darwin's eyes. "There are whispers."

"Whispers...?"

"Yes. The whispers say I will be remembered—if I am to be remembered at all—primarily for conveying upon my vessel the man who assaulted the Lord, armed only with the blunt weapon of modern biology."

Darwin shut his eyes and rode out a new wave of nausea. He would not insult his old friend by denying the potential effects of his own work, especially now that he had let Lyell look at his transmutation sketches and been cautioned by the great scientist himself that publishing his ideas threatened to do exactly as FitzRoy accused: separate religion and science permanently, to the detriment of all.

"Is that what you're doing? Are you trying to prove that God has no place here? What is your secret, Charles? You discovered something—or think you did—in the Galapagos, and have been tiptoeing around it for twenty years."

Again, Darwin would not insult FitzRoy by denying it. He said only, "How do you come to hear such things?"

"It is assumed that I share in this secret. This speculation about the origin of species, the origin of mankind in direct contradiction to God's own Word."

Darwin lay back on the divan and stared at the ceiling. "The whispers speak the truth."

Hearing this, FitzRoy drove a knuckle into his forehead and clenched his eyes shut, as if he were fighting against tears. "You have betrayed me."

"No!" Darwin cried. "This is exactly why I have published nothing on the subject, not a word, though I have written many books now."

"But you have shared the idea, with men like Charles Lyell."

"Only in the strictest of secrecy," Darwin said, but realized immediately that this could not be the case, if the whispers had spread even to FitzRoy. "I admit—it creates excitement, and this leads some to heedlessness."

"Especially among the atheistic scientific community."

"Lyell is no atheist, Robert. In fact, he finds the mechanics of my transmutation ideas invalid for that very reason."

"He is an ass, then," FitzRoy said, "picking fights just for the sheer joy of seeing feathers ruffled."

Darwin did not respond to this. The truth was that Lyell did reject the idea of selection by nature, the mechanism Darwin had finally worked out for the origin of species, but not only on religious grounds. In fact, Lyell's scientific criticisms had helped Darwin sharpen the less rigorous parts of his argument.

But what he said next he meant as absolute truth.

"Robert, I have no plans to publish this work during my lifetime. I have developed it over the years, it is true, refined it, even shared it with a like mind or two." Darwin sat up again. "But it will go with me to the grave. It would hurt too many friends—like you, but you are not the only one—and I believe my poor Emma would never survive the shame that the accusations of heresy would bring."

FitzRoy nodded and paused before saying, "Charles, I cannot share with you the specific reason why, but—you owe God your fealty. As do I."

Darwin merely stiffened. "I will avoid releasing research that may, in the ignorance of the masses, result in the besmirching of my family's name. I owe nothing to anyone or anything else but my own conscience."

"So still you arrogantly hold to your own delusions on this subject. You believe that God had no hand in the Creation of Man."

"I have not said that, and do not say it."

"But the twitch of your hand at your traitorous belly tells me you long to do exactly that."

"I refuse to answer accusations made on the basis of twitches and farts."

"But you create this theory of transmutation on the basis of sickbed dreams!"

Darwin looked incredulously at FitzRoy. "That I have shared with no man. You make a lucky guess, or else you are a demon."

"Fair enough," FitzRoy said, and took to his feet. "But I warn you, my old friend—this world and the people in it have shown me they give not a copper farthing what a noble man does in the service to his Country. So let any man beware what I will do in service to the next world, and to my Lord."

"Robert, what are you saying?"

"I am saying, dear Charles, that if you unleash this idea on the world, then the Lord God will strike you down, and as much as I love you, I will be His hammer."

Powell

In this world, there are no miracles. There is only Law.

When a child falls victim to an illness, doctors make no effort to valiantly "save" her—there is no "saving" anyone, for that means miraculously interceding in the Lawful workings of the universe. Instead, physicians join clerics in poring over books containing the Law as it is understood. These symptoms mean this disease; those symptoms mean another disorder. Some are pronounced terminal, others easily cured. Medical men work mechanically according to the books, as does the clergy.

Here the origin of species is no more mysterious than the ticking of a clock. All that stands between man and his full understanding of this part of the Law are enough evidence, specimens, corrected anomalies to illuminate how the book must be written. There is no awe; there is nothing miraculous. Species were born in particular ways, naturally, without any hand of God or divine intervention, because God is the Lawmaker in addition to standing as judge and jury, and His Laws are eternal and good.

Since God set down His Laws in nature at the beginning of time, He has rested, not taking part any more in His Creation than the audience of a play takes part in the fates of the characters on stage. If He needed to resort to miracles, that would mean that His Creation, His Laws, were flawed; therefore, believing in miracles is a sign of a lack of faith in God, of vile atheism.

In emulation of this Lawmaker God, men make decisions once and never change their minds, lest they be accused of godlessness. It matters not to anyone that man makes mistakes in his intentions and actions—a Law made in error is a contradiction in terms. The Law is the Law forever in Heaven, and so shall it be on Earth. All men stand by their first proclamations, consequences be damned. No miraculous intervention is expected from God, and so no one should expect a change of heart, an intervention of mercy, from those who believe in and would be like Him.

"God loves you. That's why He made this world for you, with everything working the way it does," the pastor wants to tell his daughter, but he has caught a chill, unusual in the middle of summer, and lost his voice.

The daughter does not understand why her father will not talk to her, or comfort her. The world is darkness to her since her eyes failed. Her small, cool hands grasp his big, warm fingers, so she knows he is there, but he will no longer speak, and this makes her weep tears of pain and frustration.

The father sees her cry, and wipes her tears, hoping this will show her that he cares, even though he cannot answer her pleas for him to say something to her, even though he cannot respond when she asks if he is angry with her for her blindness, or why God would take away her sight, or why Mama isn't with them anymore.

If he could speak, he would tell her that God made Laws, and somehow they have trespassed in violation of them, and so they are being punished, justly. There is no appeal to make, no divine intervention to beg for. They must just sit and endure their penalty, in the dark and the silence until God grants them reprieve. The Law says that people need only to repent for their crimes in order to be forgiven, but the pastor and his daughter don't know what they might have done. So they must choose: They can regret nothing, or they can regret everything they have ever done. Either way, should mercy one day come, it will feel like a miracle.

Antemeridian

The great black ape, each of his fingers the size of a man's leg, turns me over as I lie in the bottom of an enormous bowl. I am naked except for black socks and garters, and the cold porcelain of the bowl warms quickly beneath my flesh. The ape scratches his chin the way a Cambridge professor might as he pokes my back, then grunts to himself and writes something on a banana leaf.

I am able to turn myself right again in the curve of the bowl, and see that another ape, this one with silver hair around its ears, has joined the black ape. Silver takes the pipe from his mouth and points the stem at me, hooting something to Black that makes them both chuckle. Black shakes his head ruefully, and lifts me out of the bowl by my stockinged foot.

He grunts out to a manic Rhesus Monkey which is just larger than I and comes scurrying across the table. With a series of snorts, Black shakes me by way of instruction to the Rhesus, and the monkey understands. I am dropped onto the wooden table and the monkey drags me by that same foot—the garter breaks and the stocking slips off in his hand, but he tosses the sock aside and commences dragging me again—over to a cage lined with straw and containing two other men, naked except one wears a gray bowler-hat and the other a striped nightcap.

179

I am pushed roughly into the giant cage and sit on the only available seat, a red velvet ottoman. Nightcap says, "A bit disappointed, aren't they?"

Bowler-hat offers me a wan smile and says, "They just can't—"

The black moon of the giant ape's head eclipses the room as he peers into the cage, snorts disdainfully, and writes another note on his banana leaf before ending his occultation of our light and air.

Bowler-hat lets out a sad laugh and shakes his head. "They just can't believe it," he says.

Down House, 1858

The letter from Lyell lay on Darwin's desk, but he had not finished reading it once it introduced the twenty-page treatise enclosed in the envelope: "On the Tendency of Varieties to Depart Indefinitely from the Original Type," by a young naturalist named Wallace, of whom Darwin—or Lyell, for that matter—had never heard a word spoken.

But Wallace had written, in succinct prose ready for publication, the entire foundation of natural selection as the mechanism for the origin of species. The short paper missed the mark in a number of places—Darwin did not truck with the idea of a social utopia as the *telos* of development—and it did not include anything approaching the detail of Darwin's own 231-page manuscript Lyell had read, but it was identical in the essentials to the ideas Darwin had been hiding since reading Malthus, and making the vital connection, nineteen years earlier.

He had slaved over barnacles, watched his daughter die, and taken the water cure for his chronic stomach complaint. He had not published his theory. He had wasted the greatest opportunity for scientific advancement and personal achievement anyone could have wished for, all on the basis of weakness and fear. Now this Wallace—this brave young man who sent his paper unsolicited to an unknown scientific eminence, caring not for his own or his family's reputation in church or in society—would be seen as the true progenitor of Darwin's idea.

He could not in any kind of good conscience rush to publish his work now, although Darwin was a highly respected scientific man and Wallace an unknown and could take the rug from beneath the younger man's feet; no, Wallace had claimed the moral right to publish the theory with his bravery, and Darwin would not cheat him, although it meant he would be reduced to—

He stopped himself. *Reduced?* He would be *reduced* by another man's achievements? That was FitzRoy speaking.

He could feel his gorge rise, ready to unload his breakfast once again, but he let out a sailor's swear—for the first time in fifteen years—and forced his meal back down. He pushed Wallace's treatise out of the way, reached for his pen and paper and dashed off a letter to Lyell, asking for advice. He called Parslow to catch the postman and get it out that very morning.

      CS   CS   CS

In less than a week, the reply came from Lyell. He agreed with Darwin that Wallace had the moral high ground, but also agreed with him that a man of Darwin's distinction would be heeded much more by the scientific community than would a complete unknown currently traveling in Malay. For the sake of the theory, and for the sake of courtesy and morality, their papers would both be read before the Linnaean Society in July, giving Wallace exposure to the world of science he never could have dreamed of, and giving Darwin the chance to stake his claim as the discoverer of natural selection.

Moving quickly, Darwin fished the packet of his transmutation manuscript out of its hiding place in the bowels of his
desk, grabbed a piece of paper, and began working like a soul
fighting for its immortality.

Antemeridian

Something has happened to my body. My bones seem made of wet powder. My skin is thinner than an onion's. Erasmus shatters my forearm when he embraces me. I slip and fall against the table, staving in my ribs and filling the room with bone dust.

"You are old," Erasmus says. He is older than I, but looks as he did when he was on the rowing team. How old was he then? Two and twenty, if that? "You are old. You must rest."

Blood trickles in my veins, my heart barely forceful enough to create a pulse. My beard is brittle, and pieces break off like sugar cane as Erasmus sits down what is left of me in a leather armchair by the window. I feel my desiccated form mold to the chair, skin crinkling as it is deformed.

"Water," Erasmus says, and gently lifts a goblet to my lips. I swallow, but I can feel the liquid seep out through worn spots in my jaw and throat, and make a puddle on my wool breeches.

"There is nothing for it," I try to say, but all that comes from my lips is an arid whisper. Erasmus shakes his head at me to show that he does not understand me, or does not agree, or does not want this ancient specimen in his parlor. My eyes are drying up in their sockets, and the lids will no longer close against their papery surface.

I want to shout for help, but my tongue, my teeth, all have lost cohesion and broken away, turned to talcum as I try to work them. I am cracking, crumbling, dust and hard pieces of dead flesh rolling down my body like rocks in a desert land-slide.

Erasmus continues to watch me, unmoving, dust-pan at the ready.

Wallace

In this world, it is survival of the fittest. There is no mercy or special dispensation for age, reputation, or good intentions; any creature that will live long enough to reproduce must fight for its very existence against other creatures desiring the same resources.

The lumbering dinosaur shivers in the gray rain, trying to protect its eggs from this changing, cold world. But the small, fur-laden mammal darts between the behemoth's legs, its embryos perfectly warm as they develop inside her womb.

The tortoise beats the hare, not because he is faster, but because the hare neglects to run, and running is what wins the race. Then, at the finish, the tortoise eats all the food, and the late-arriving hare starves to death, for hares and tortoises survive on the same sustenance.

The sea-captain stays with his sinking ship, even as there is room on the life-boat next to the naturalist, because the captain's honor demands it of him. His honor will not be spread among the living; it will be drowned with him, and by definition only the dishonorable will survive, and spread their evil among the generations to come.

On occasion, however, the fading dinosaur will fall directly on top of the vigorous mammal, and crush it; the hare will regain his strength enough to steal from the tortoise; the mast of the sinking ship will catch the life-boat and drag it under with it.

This is not survival for the unfit, but it brings satisfaction nonetheless.

Oxford, 1860

"… I unhesitatingly affirm my preference for the ape," Huxley retorted to the Reverend Wilberforce's taunt about Huxley's ancestors, and brought the house down.

Some men wept with laughter, while others jumped to their feet to shout angry epithets at their opponents in what was not meant to be a discussion on Darwin's "theory of evolution" at all, but a lecture by John William Draper on the intellectual development of Europe. The old man planted in the middle seat of a middle row—sixty-five, at least, maybe much older, but for any age presenting a pale and shabby appearance even in his rear-admiral's uniform—would not have come if he had known such a debate were going to break out.

Robert FitzRoy had come to Oxford the day before to give a talk himself, about barometers and weather forecasting, but all of that was forgotten now as his brain latched on to what men were saying was "Truth," as if science could ever discover such a thing. He had been a scientific man all his life, and had never found any Truth at all, only learned facts and taken measurements. All of this geology and paleontology was rubbish if it made the Earth seem a day over six thousand years old. Hadn't these overeducated fools read *Omphalos*, the landmark work by Gosse that showed how God had created these very fossils and geological artifacts to give the world the *appearance* of great age?

The chattering of excited men continued, even height-ened, as they called out the accursed name again and again and again:

"Darwin says clearly that—"

"If Darwinism is to work, we must—"

"I wish that Mister Darwin himself were here—"

"Darwin! Darwin! *Darwin!*"

The old admiral stood and stepped onto his chair, raising a leather-bound book above him. "Charles Darwin cannot tell you the Truth! You must look in here! This is the Truth—in here! *In here!*" he shouted—screamed—with all of his strength, thrusting the Bible as high as he could for all to see.

But his voice, which once could be heard across a mile of open sea, was no longer powerful enough to wrench the room from its frenzy. No one took notice of him but one young man, by the looks of him an undergraduate, who stood in the row before FitzRoy's. The admiral looked down at the stu-dent kindly and said, "The Truth. This is the Truth. Not Dar-win and monkeys."

The student said, "Your father *must* have been a monkey, the way an old ape like you climbs a chair," and, with a snort, turned away.

Gosse

In this world, the Earth appears to have existed for an almost unfathomable expanse of time. Eons, millions of years, thousands of millions. Fossils are buried in rock in ways that suggest waves of catastrophe, mass extinctions, oceans turned to deserts turned to marshland turned to oceans again. Present species seem to have developed from earlier, simpler creatures that no longer exist. The Earth exhibits through its geology the memory of deep time.

This is an illusion.

The Earth is in fact less than six thousand years old, and was created exactly as described in the Book of Genesis. Rivers then are rivers now. Mountains have not changed, in size or position or in any other way. Every animal in every species is in form and function exactly as it was at the moment of Creation. Humans, too, have remained exactly as Adam was first Created, down to his *omphalos*, his navel. The navels of Adam and Eve make for clear, unimpeachable evidence that they were born of women, conceived and nourished in the womb in the manner with which we are familiar. This conclusion is as clear as it is false.

In this world, evidence is no basis for belief. All we know is what we see of this moment, at this moment, *in* this moment. The collections and accretions of a billion years can be known only because they are beheld *now*. Memories are experienced only *in the present*—none of them are sure to refer to anything that actually happened. The past is as unchartable as the future; there is no point in trying to surmise what might once have taken place, even in one's own life, any more than there is in guessing what will happen in some vague and unknowable time to come.

Jails are emptied as the courts realize that all testimony is without value. Witnesses are speaking of their mental formations at that moment, not relating memories that have anything to do with the alleged incident at hand. Fingerprints as well are no sign of a suspect's presence at the scene of the crime: Whorls on a murder weapon are there *now*. We can know nothing of them being placed there at the time of the murder.

Indeed, the sorry man in the courtroom dock, chains around his wrists and ankles, is committing no crime at all. Who can say what he *has done*? Those are words without meaning, worthless speculations about a world no one can see or experience in any way. It is like executing a man for something he *might do*, an absurdity. The moment's innocent are released.

In families, anniversaries are not celebrated, photographs are not bothered with. School lessons are not remembered, no matter how it may seem; knowledge only is or is not—how could it be otherwise? This results in people going about their days without worry over results. But also it results in no feelings of accomplishment, no congratulations for jobs well done. Any effort was an illusion; the job is now completed; who can say who achieved what in some unreachable "past"?

The sea-captain and the naturalist were never friends. They never rode together in South America, never dined as equals in the captain's cabin, never wrote each other notes of affection and admiration, never shared souls. All pieces of evidence to the contrary, including their own memories, are just chimærical epiphenomena, phantoms that exist in this moment only and have nothing to do with friendship, or connection, or years spent living as brothers.

And lovers, too, must change tactics. Like anything else in this world, love can never be proved. Scientist husbands and their pious wives must agree to disagree, because nothing can ever change; exhortation and cajoling achieves nothing the other party does not feel the whim to do anyway. There is no begging for explanations, but there is also no forgiveness. There are only the feelings *now*, love or its absence. It is simple. It is cruel.

Antemeridian

My mother and I sit at opposite ends of a very long dining table. She died when I was but eight years old, and the years under the ground have not been gentle. Her flesh is mostly worn away, but where skin remains it is yellow and right against her skull.

"Father said you would be back," I tell her.

The empty eye sockets peer back at me. She speaks to me—her mandible moves up and down, still connected by sinew to her skull—but no sound comes out, her larynx long since rotted away. But her words are clear: *I want my dinner.*

"There will be no dinner for the dead," I tell her, repeating my father's words.

She rises from her seat, floats above it, her dun-colored graveclothes worm-eaten and wilted. Her jaw opens as she glides over the table towards me, the bones of her arms and hands extended for an embrace.

I am hungry, Bobby. Feed me.

"I don't know what that means!"

I remain transfixed, paralyzed, as my mother's corpse drifts to me, to give me the final kiss she never could in life. She is huge in my eyes now, overwhelming me, and I can smell nothing but the sourness of an approaching grave.

Down House, 1865

The post, as usual, was voluminous. The carrier had given to leaving sacks with Parslow, picking them up the next day as he dropped off a new load. Invitations to the famous Mister Darwin, sometimes to "Doctor" Darwin, offers of samples, requests for samples, praise, threats, monographs, postcards from all corners of the globe, and, often, letters from his children, which was the only post he opened before luncheon and a nap.

"This is a happy day, Joseph! I have only a few acknowledgments to make, and then my final manuscript is ready to be seen by other eyes. *The Descent of Man*. That should get the last of the rabble shaken up, eh? We will need our own mail-cart for all the angry post that will bring."

Hearing no response to his witticism from his servant, Darwin looked up to see a grave expression on Parslow's face. Today he held one envelope separate from the others. It was bordered in the black trim of mourning stationery.

"Oh, keep good cheer—none of us can escape the Reaper, my friend," Darwin said with a sad chuckle. If it had been anyone in the family, he would have heard long before the post delivered the news, and so he could make a small jest. "No doubt it is one of the more advanced members of our Royal

Society who has passed on, opening an endowed chair some-where for a new star in the firmament. More happiness than sadness, I'm afraid, in that equation."

Parslow moved to say something, but instead chose to re-main silent, still stiffly holding the letter by its edge.

Darwin sighed. "Well then, from whom do we hear to-day?"

Parslow hesitated, then said, "The widow FitzRoy, sir."

It was as if a trap door had swung open below Darwin, for the world fell away for a moment, leaving him weightless, breathless, hanging. But as he had for fifteen years, Parslow brought him back around with a firm slap on the back and a hard shake of his shoulders. Darwin nodded in thanks and took the envelope, opening it and quickly reading that FitzRoy had passed only a few days earlier; the funeral was to commence the next morning in London. Of course Darwin would not attend, as he left his home these days for hardly anything; and he had not seen his old captain the past eight years. But he said to Parslow, "Have flowers sent, Joseph, if you would. Tele-graph our condolences. Offer any support, material or other-wise. Whatever is appropriate on these occasions—ask Mrs. Darwin if you need more direction."

Of course Parslow needed no such thing, but Darwin's mouth was working without real reference to his brain. Pars-low nodded, and left his employer sitting at his desk, morning sunlight falling across unseeing eyes, but before he had reached the stairs, Darwin called out: "Joseph! Do we know... *how* we have come to lose Admiral FitzRoy? Was it his heart, so over-taxed these many years?"

"God be with him, sir, he has—he was..." Parslow took in a deep breath. "He took his own life, sir."

"I see," Darwin said, fading again. "Thank you, Joseph."

Parslow bowed formally and retreated again towards the stairs, leaving Darwin to stare at the sheaf of paper before him, his last word on evolution ready to be bundled and sent off. He had long dreamed of this moment, the moment when he could relax and no longer face a world that disagreed with him; it was all going to be in books now, for the new generations to argue over.

But he had dreamed of this moment in other ways as well. Sometimes, between the unicorns and the flying tortoises, he dreamed that FitzRoy would finally accept his family's inheritance, finally plunge into darkness. The Lord God would not break His loyal and loving servant's fall, would let him plummet all the way to Hell for his suicide. The descent of man, indeed.

Against wet eyes, Darwin smiled. It made him glad that so many correspondents told him that he had killed God. It meant he had saved his Captain.

Without speaking to Emma or Parslow or anyone else in the house, Darwin finished his last page and placed it on top of the pile. The work was done. Robert FitzRoy was dead, in a universe without God, or Heaven, or Hell.

There was nothing more to dream.

Acknowledgments

This novel would not have been possible without the guidance and information provided by these excellent resources: Adrian Desmond and James Moore's *Darwin: The Life of a Tormented Evolutionist*; Stephen Jay Gould's *Leonardo's Mountain of Clams and the Diet of Worms: Essays on Natural History*; Richard Lee Marks's *Three Men of the* Beagle; Peter Nichols's *Evolution's Captain: The Dark Fate of the Man Who Sailed Charles Darwin around the World*; and Michael White and John Gribbin's *Darwin: A Life in Science*.

I owe a special debt of gratitude to Michael Martone, Dr. Wendy Rawlings, Joel Brouwer, Kate Bernheimer, Dr. Stephen Tomlinson, Alissa Nutting, Andrew Farkas, Carl Peterson, Rachel Mack, Tara Goejden, Nick Pincumbe, the University of Alabama and its librarians, the Tuscaloosa Public Library, the editors of the online Oxford English Dictionary, and David Leff, curator of the indispensable AboutDarwin.com, as well as proofer, editor and wife *extraordinaire*, Ann Hoade. And, of course, to Charles Darwin and Robert Fitz-Roy, two men who dreamed hard to find the source of life, as well as its purpose.

Alex Haber

About the Author

SEAN HOADE lives near the University of Alabama, where he earned an MFA in fiction (after a degree in philosophy and cognitive science from Indiana University), and where he now teaches classes on creative writing, English composition, American literature, Buddhism, zombies, superheroes, the Apocalypse, and more. He is the author of the novel *Ain't that America* and has had fiction and poetry published in magazines such as *Carve* and *horse less review* as well as in the Wisdom Books anthology *You Are Not Here and Other Works of Buddhist Fiction*. He welcomes interesting e-mail at *seanhoade@gmail.com*.

Made in the USA